AN
ESCAPE
IN
TIME

SALLY NICHOLLS

First published in the UK in 2021 by Nosy Crow Ltd

The Crow's Nest, 14 Baden Place
Crosby Row, London, SE1 1YW

Nosy Crow and associated logos are trademarks and/or registered
trademarks of Nosy Crow Ltd.

Text copyright © Sally Nicholls, 2021
Cover copyright © Isabelle Follath, 2021
Inside illustrations copyright © Rachael Dean, 2021

ISBN: 978 1 78800 124 3

A CIP catalogue record for this book is available from the British Library.

Printed and bound in Great Britain by Clays Ltd, Elcograf S.p.A.

Papers used by Nosy Crow are made from wood grown in sustainable forests.

MIX
Paper from
responsible sources
FSC® C018072
www.fsc.org

1 3 5 7 9 10 8 6 4 2

www.nosycrow.com

CHAPTER ONE
THE APPEARANCE
IN A HALLWAY

In the hallway of Aunt Joanna's house, there was a magic mirror.

Huge, gold-framed and mysterious, there it hung, looking innocent.

Ruby Pilgrim *glared* at it.

"Just look at that!" she said indignantly. "Sitting there like a lump of glass! Like it's just – a reflecting thing or something!"

"It is a reflecting thing," said her brother, Alex. "It's just … sometimes it's a time-travelling thing as well."

Because sometimes, the mirror showed another reflection, of another Applecott House in another time. Last summer, they'd gone back to 1912 and helped save a priceless golden cup. Ruby still hadn't sorted out how she felt about that. She'd hated it and she'd loved it, all at the same time. It had been wonderful … and really, really frightening. For quite a lot of it, she'd been certain they were going to be stuck in 1912 forever, and would probably have to go and live in a workhouse or something and…

It still made her go cold to remember it.

But then at Christmas they'd come back to Applecott House, and this time they'd stepped back into 1872. They'd landed in a gloriously Victorian Christmas, with plum pudding, and ice skating on the lake, and charades. There'd been danger there, too, but most of it had been simply wonderful.

Ruby didn't like to admit it, but she missed it. All this last year, in a busy, noisy secondary school in a little northern town, where the only things anyone seemed to care about was what sort of shoes you wore, and what sort of music you liked, and who fancied who ... Ruby had found her thoughts tugging back again and again to that other time, where magic existed and wishes came true and girls her age wore pinafores and petticoats, and didn't have to worry about things like eyeliner and tweezers and shaving their legs. The past, though she would never have said so out loud, had been rather restful.

But now it was half-term. They'd come back to Aunt Joanna's house for their cousin's wedding, and were staying on a couple of days so that their parents could help Aunt Joanna with the repairs to the house. And this time...

This time, she kept looking at the glass, hoping it would change.

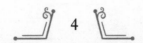

"I was so sure it would open again," she said. "But why would it? It's not like we're anyone special really, are we?"

"I suppose not," said Alex sadly.

They both looked back at the mirror.

Which was reflecting another room.

"Oh!" said Ruby.

The room in the mirror was, very definitely, not in Applecott House. It was clearly a much grander place, with blue walls and tall windows showing a large formal garden. There was an elaborate-looking fireplace behind it, with enormous golden candlesticks on the mantel. Ruby didn't have time to properly take this in, though, because all at once a person appeared in the frame.

It was a very, *very* superior-looking person, in a long, loose gown, of the sort that needs an awful lot of artifice to look natural. At least, Ruby supposed it did; the person had a very narrow waist, which *must* mean she was wearing a corset, and her hair, though loose-ish, was *elaborately* loose, with three curls hanging *here*, and a big bouffy bit *here*, and it was a very unnatural-looking greyish-white, as though someone had covered it in powder.

Her cap was complicated too, with lots of lacy bits, and there was more lace round her neck, and ribbons on her sleeves, and what looked like little roses on her shoes. She looked like a very rich person who had spent an hour this morning dressing herself up to look like a very expensive milkmaid.

She appeared to be in a state of panic. She was shouting at someone outside the frame and pulling at them. Alex and Ruby couldn't hear what she said, but she seemed to be pleading with someone just out of sight. She stumbled backwards, and the person was revealed. He was a boy about Ruby's age or a little older, dressed in a blue suit complete with waistcoat, short, tight trousers that came to his knees, white stockings and blue shoes with shiny silver buckles. He had shaggy brown hair that touched his shoulders and he too looked terrified. He was shouting and crying hysterically. His hands flapped in the air in front of him and his mother grabbed them, pulling them down, and then —

And then they stumbled sideways against the mirror.

And vanished.

"Where have they gone?" said Ruby. She scrambled off the window seat. "They should be here! Shouldn't they? Shouldn't they have come here? Where are they?"

"How should I know?" said Alex. Then: "Look!"

Another person had appeared in the mirror. It was a girl who could have been anywhere from about fifteen to nineteen. She was dressed more simply, in a long, plain dress, and her hair, though curled, was less artfully arranged. She ran up to the mirror and her eyes widened in shock. She could see them – Alex was sure of it. She was staring at *him*.

They both, almost without thinking, moved closer to the mirror – so close that they could have reached out and touched the girl if they'd wanted. It was strangely intimate, the three of them there looking so intently at each other, separated only by the glass. Ruby hardly dared to move in case the girl vanished. Who was she? What was happening?

And then, suddenly, the girl in the mirror flinched and looked back over her shoulder. There it was – the same look of terror on her face. Someone else was there – men, more roughly dressed than

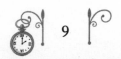

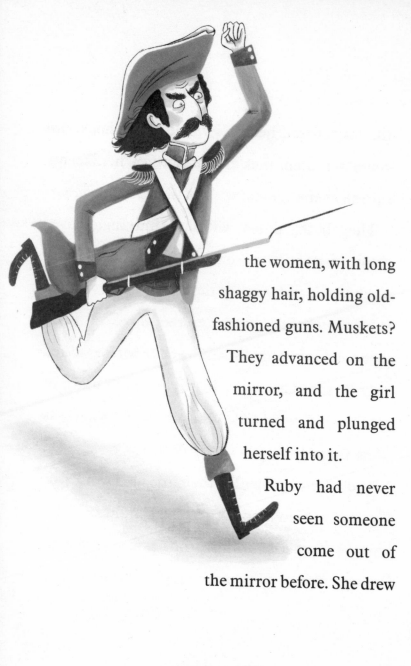

the women, with long shaggy hair, holding old-fashioned guns. Muskets? They advanced on the mirror, and the girl turned and plunged herself into it.

Ruby had never seen someone come out of the mirror before. She drew back in instinctive panic. The girl's arms and hands appeared, then her head, then her fingers gripped round their arms with unexpected vigour.

"Hey!" Ruby yelled. "What are you *doing*?"

But it was too late. Because now the mirror was sucking *them* in.

Ruby cried, "Let go!"

And then they landed on the floor with a *thump*.

"Ow!" said Alex.

"What did you do that for?" Ruby yelled.

She sat up, rubbing the back of her head. The three of them – Alex, Ruby and the young woman – were lying on a tiled floor in the hallway of what must be Applecott House. But how strange it looked!

Everything, except the basic shape of the room, was different. The windows were small and diamond-paned and there were many more of them; there were oil paintings on the wall and no furniture in the hallway at all, except for a small table with a little silver dish and a wide-brimmed black hat on it. The front doors looked different, and the door to the downstairs toilet was missing. There were no light fittings, not even for gas. No radiators (the room was rather cold). No plug sockets. Nothing looked familiar and the whole place looked *new*.

Applecott House was Georgian. It had looked old for as long as Alex could remember. Worn stonework on the outside walls of the house. Worn paint on the back door (the front was kept nice for the guests at Aunt Joanna's bed and breakfast). Old glass, and old pipes, and old, smooth bannisters – old everything.

This house looked new. The walls were freshly papered with green wallpaper. The bannisters were clearly made of new wood, and so were the window frames. It was disorientating. It smelled of fresh autumn air, and candle wax, and wood polish, and smoke.

"Good Lord! What devilry is this? More of you!"

It was a man's voice. The children turned. Standing behind them – staring – were the grand woman and the boy from the mirror, looking, if

13

anything, grander and more overdressed than ever in person. Next to them, looking utterly astonished, was a short, stocky man, with red hair and the most extraordinary red side whiskers, like mad overgrown sideburns. He was youngish – perhaps early twenties – and not fat exactly, but his waistcoat was definitely too tight, and his stomach bulged out of the bottom. He was dressed entirely, completely in black, and his face was round and red and amiable, though his mouth was open in amazement.

The boy cried, "Mademoiselle Crouchman!" in a French accent, and the young woman, who was sitting on the floor next to Ruby, scrambled to feet, crying, "My lord! My lady!" Unlike the boy, her voice sounded properly English, like she'd been speaking it all her life. "My apologies, sir, I do not believe we have been introduced."

The whiskery man gave a brisk bow.

"Frederick Pilgrim at your service," he said.

Alex and Ruby looked at each other. A Pilgrim! Family!

"I am – excuse me, madam, I am all astonishment. It is not usual in these parts for gentlefolk – or, indeed, any folk at all – to travel by means of a looking glass. What manner of creatures are you? If you be devils, I assure you I am a gentleman of the cloth, and I will undertake to cast you out by any means possible. Although –" and here he almost smiled – "I confess, I do know exactly know how one performs an exorcism, the existence of demons not being a matter of much consequence in Suffolk."

"Demons!" said the grand woman, drawing herself to her full height. She had the same French accent as the boy. "I assure you, sir, I am no demon. I am the Countess d'Allonette, and I demand you explain yourself at once. How came you to own my looking glass? To what purpose did you transport us here? Are you a part of this dreadful revolution? Explain yourself, I insist!"

"Oh!" said Ruby. "You're the witch!" She grabbed Alex's arm in excitement. "Don't you remember? Aunt Joanna said a witch made the mirror magic to escape getting guillotined in the

French Revolution. She said this Countess was about to be arrested, and she just stepped into a mirror and disappeared!"

"A witch!" The Countess turned an icy expression on to Ruby. "I am a noblewoman of France, a country now sadly overrun by barbarians. What mean you by such remarks?"

"Well, *somebody* made the mirror magic," said Alex. "And it wasn't us."

There was a small noise behind them. Alex turned. The young woman – Mademoiselle Crouchman – was clearing her throat.

"I beg your pardon, my lady," she said. "But I believe it may have been me."

CHAPTER TWO
A MEETING
WITH A WITCH

There was a short, stunned pause. Then Miss Crouchman swayed.

"My apologies," she said. "I feel – a little—"

Frederick caught her hand.

"The lady is faint," he said. He raised his voice.

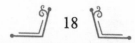

"Ho, there! Some assistance, please!"

A maid appeared. To Alex's surprise, she looked about Ruby's age, with raw red hands, a thin, rough-looking face, and fine black hair scraped under a cap.

Frederick said, "Helen! I wish you would fetch us some refreshments for our guests. And some wine for the lady, who is feeling faint."

The girl stared, then bobbed her head, said, "Of course, sir," and disappeared back into the kitchen.

Frederick took Miss Crouchman's arm.

"If you would allow me, madam. My drawing room is just through here. Perhaps we might sit and take some tea and you – and your mistress –"

a glance at the Countess, who was looking furious – "might tell me what's amiss. I own I long to know who you are and what concerns you with my poor parish."

The Countess drew herself up to her full height.

"Mademoiselle Crouchman! Control yourself!" she said. Then, graciously to Frederick, she said, "Naturally, we would be delighted to accept. Camille! Come!" And she swept out of the hallway and through the door, the boy following behind her.

Frederick looked at the children and made a face clearly intended to mean "Phew!" Alex giggled. He liked this man who must be some relation of his.

"Now, Miss Crouchman," he said, "do not distress yourself. I shall endeavour to assist you and your friends in whatever way I can. Believe me, truly, when I say it will be as much a duty as a pleasure."

Miss Crouchman nodded. "It is just... It is so very strange!"

"Indeed it is." Frederick squeezed her hand. "Come! Let us share our stories, and surely we shall find the answer to all our questions."

They went through into the drawing room, which had pale blue walls, a little coffee table, a green sofa and chairs with little legs, and a bookcase with glass doors. It looked rather more girly than Alex expected, but old-fashioned houses often looked like that. This room was rather colder than was comfortable, but there was a small fire burning in the grate, which helped.

The maid – Helen – reappeared with a small glass of wine for Miss Crouchman and another for the Countess, who drank it with her icy expression. The boy, Camille, sat close beside her with rather a closed expression on his face. He was still very white.

"Now," said Frederick, when they had finished. "Let us all tell our tales and see if we can come to an understanding of our situation. I shall begin. I am a poor clergyman, of the parish of Dalton in Suffolk. I bought the looking glass in the hallway

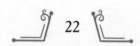

from a dealer in Ipswich, who told me it had come from the King's palace in Versailles. Naturally, I did not believe him, but perchance he was correct?" He looked enquiringly at the Countess.

Camille said, "We were in Versailles but a moment ago. How –?"

"It's a time-travelling mirror," said Ruby. "I *told* you. Look – what's the date today?"

"'Tis … now, let me see … the twentieth of September, 1795," said Frederick.

The Countess gasped. "Nay! 'Tis not possible! Why, 'twas but March 1794 when we left France!" She rounded on Mademoiselle Crouchman. "What witchcraft is this? How can one travel from spring to autumn without passing through summer between? How can one leap across a whole year without touching it?"

"Indeed I long to know," Frederick agreed. "Would not one bump into houses and people as one travelled through the months?"

"What? No! It's not like that at all!" said Ruby. "It's just – it's like stepping through a door. And then you step out here. I don't know what happens to all the years in between."

"Perchance Miss Crouchman can enlighten us."

"Oh!" Miss Crouchman shook her head. "As to that, sir, 'tis as great a mystery to me as it is to you."

"Well! Let us not concern ourselves with the wherefores before we have dispensed with the

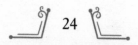

whats," said Frederick, which Alex thought meant *Let's not worry about why until we've figured out what has happened*. "My lady?" He inclined his head. "May I beg you to tell us your tale?"

"Naturally, you may." The Countess drew herself up and seemed about to begin, when the door opened and the little servant girl appeared again, carrying a tray with a teapot and teacups on it.

There was a pause while Frederick fussed around pouring cups of tea and offering everyone little cakes. The tea was weak and rather disgusting, and the cakes tasted mostly of raisins. At last, when everyone was served, Frederick bobbed his head to the Countess and said, "And now, my lady.

Let us begin."

The Countess sat up a little straighter. She looked all around the drawing room to make sure she had their full attention. Then she said, "My name is Jeanne d'Aubenny, Countess d'Allonette. This is my son, Camille d'Aubenny, Lord Connett. And this is Camille's English governess, Eleanor Crouchman, a very good sort of woman."

Alex glanced at the governess, Eleanor. She was looking at the floor, her hands clenched. He wondered how old she was.

"Naturally, the situation in France has been causing much distress to our friends and ourselves." She meant the French Revolution, Alex realised. He didn't know much about the

French Revolution. There was the old joke: "The peasants are revolting!" And something about the Queen telling people to eat cake. But one thing he did know was the revolutionaries chopped off the heads of the aristocrats with guillotines. Was that what had been happening to the Countess's friends?

Was that what those men had wanted to do to the Countess?

"Since the death of the Count, Camille and I have been part of the Queen's court at Versailles. In recent months, we have been working to help our friends to safety."

"You mean you were a counter-revolutionary?" Ruby perked up. "Did you sneak around after

dark getting people out of the palace? Did you have a musket?"

"What an abominable notion!" The Countess looked horrified. "Naturally, I did nothing of the sort. No, I merely … passed messages and made introductions, nothing less."

"Like a spy for the resistance," said Alex, fascinated.

The Countess bristled. "Nay! I assure you, nothing so vulgar."

"Vulgar! Nay! I think it everything that is brave and noble!" said Frederick enthusiastically. The Countess twitched her skirt with a gesture of irritation, but a prim look of self-satisfaction crept around her lips.

"As to that, it was nothing," she said. "But evidently the soldiers of the revolution did not agree. This very afternoon, they burst into our rooms, determined to drag us off to the Bastille, and from there –"

She paused dramatically.

"The guillotine!" said Ruby.

"Just so. We screamed and fought, but there was nothing to do. Just as we thought all hope was lost, I happened to glance at my looking glass and saw that the reflection had altered, so that it showed another room and place. Naturally, I assumed it was a secret door, placed there for our escape. I grasped Camille's arm and stepped into the looking glass. And found myself here."

She waved a dismissive hand at Eleanor and Alex and Ruby. "I know not who these children are, or what this child's mother thinks to have her go about half dressed."

"They're *trousers*," said Ruby. "I'm just as dressed as Camille is!"

"As to that," said Frederick hastily. "Perhaps it is time for Miss Crouchman to speak."

He looked enquiringly at Eleanor, who drew in a deep breath and nodded. She was still rather pale, but her voice was steady.

"My name is Eleanor Crouchman," she said. "I am a lady of modest income but respectable birth. My mother died when I was a child, and my father when I was fifteen; for the past two years, I have worked in Versailles as an English governess to the young baron."

The baron? Alex supposed she must mean Camille. Posh people did have lots of confusing titles he remembered – like Prince William also being the Duke of Cambridge.

"Ever since I was a young child I have known that I was different. There have been many strange incidents – once, a carriage my mother and I were in overturned dramatically yet we found ourselves a full twenty feet from the wreckage with no ill effects. On another occasion, when I was not seven years old, I was filled with such fury over a petty injustice of childhood that I did cause a tree in my father's garden to burst into flames.

I believe it is said to run in my family – my grandmother was just the same, and there was a distant cousin who was said to have put out a fire with only the power of his mind. Naturally, it was very distressing, and I tried as best I could to hide my powers."

"Indeed, I knew nothing of it," said

the Countess. She looked down her nose at Eleanor. "What think you of this, Mr Pilgrim? Surely it is the work of the devil?"

"Ah, well, as to that." Frederick smiled at Eleanor. "All of the examples our friend has given – with – ahem – perhaps the exception of the tree, which one can overlook as the natural excitement of childhood – seem to have been acts of virtue. I cannot believe that the devil would choose to put out fires and save children from overturned carriages. Think you it is a thing of evil, Miss Crouchman?"

"I am certain it is not," said Eleanor. "I know not what it is, but I believe it is a force for good. As evidenced by what happened today. I have never been more frightened than when those men burst into the room. I was sure all hope was lost. I was filled with a blind and panicked terror, I looked wildly around the room, hoping for escape – and imagine my surprise when I saw another room reflected in my lady's looking glass! And, oh! When the Countess and Camille stepped into the glass and disappeared! But when I myself looked into the glass, all I could see were these children." She gestured to Alex and Ruby. "And then, as the men pursuing me came closer, I was filled with a strange certainty that these children were necessary for our happiness. I reached out my hands – through the glass – I took hold of them – and then here I was on the

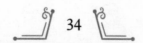

floor of your hallway. My apologies, sir," she said, bobbing her head in his direction. "I am all abasement. I declare I know not why my magic has chosen you or your house for our sanctuary."

"Oh, pish!" Frederick waved his hand. "To have strangers step out of a looking glass! 'Tis the greatest excitement of my life. I would not have missed it for anything! But now I feel we come to it. For who, my little miss and master, are you?"

Alex blinked. Who *were* they? What a question! How could they possibly explain themselves?

But Ruby had no such worries.

"I'm Ruby Pilgrim," she said. "And this is my brother, Alex. We come from two hundred years in your future. Our Great-Aunt Joanna lives in

Applecott House – we're probably your great-great-great-great-great-great-great-grandchildren or something."

"Two hundred years in the future!" Frederick clapped his hands together. "Oh! Is it not wonderful? Is it not monstrous curious?"

"It's completely bonkers," Ruby agreed. "We've been through the mirror before and every time we have these mad adventures. I don't know why. The first time it was because we wished on a witch in a bottle. I mean, maybe we did. I'm not sure. Alex had this witch in a bottle, and he wished he could save our aunt's house – it's a long story – and then we went through time and we *did* save it."

"But to what purpose are you here now?" Eleanor asked.

Ruby shrugged. "Search me," she said.

"I think there probably is a reason," Alex said slowly. "The other times, it was like we had a job to do – there was this thing that needed doing, and the mirror wouldn't open until we'd done it. So maybe there's something here too – we need to do something, and then we'll be able to go home."

"I believe you must help us," said Eleanor. "In fact, I am certain of it."

"Help you do what, though?" said Ruby.

And Eleanor said, "Help us to find our home."

CHAPTER THREE
A MEETING WITH A DANGEROUS WOMAN

There was a small silence.

Then Frederick asked, "You have nowhere to go?"

"Indeed we do not," said the Countess. "We had planned to smuggle ourselves out of the country

… my jewels were to be sent on with my servants, but, alas … we were surprised…"

"My dear lady!" said Frederick.

"Maybe they could stay with you?" Ruby said brightly. "What? Why not? He's a vicar, isn't it? Vicars are supposed to be nice to people!"

"Yes, but you can't just ask him to let three strangers live with him!" said Alex.

"Indeed we are supposed to care for those in our parish," said Frederick. "But – forgive me – I am a poor clergyman. I do not believe I could keep her ladyship in the manner to which she is accustomed, even if she *wished* to stay with me, which is by no means obvious. Do you not have friends or relations in England already?"

"Naturally, we would not wish to presume upon your hospitality," said the Countess. "But indeed I know not where my friends and relations are. I do not even know if they are alive. I have been whisked out of all society for a full half-year! I do not understand how this is possible. Why have we been brought *here*...?" She looked around her in bewilderment.

"I *told* you," said Ruby. (She hadn't, thought Alex privately.) "You can only travel to places where the mirror's been. If it got sold to Frederick, then you have to go to Frederick's house. Anyway, why should Frederick have to look after you like you're a countess? Why don't you get a job? Everyone else has to."

The Countess looked scandalised.

"A *job*? My dear child! A veritable Mary Wollstonecraft!"

"Seriously, though," said Ruby.

But just then, the door behind them opened. It was the little maid, Helen.

"Miss Broderick and Mrs Broderick, sir,"

"Oh!" Frederick's face lit up. "Show them in! Show them in! Miss Broderick." He turned to the Countess with a confidential expression on his face. "She is the dearest, sweetest creature alive! We are engaged to be married – I must introduce you at once! Although..." He lowered his voice. "Perhaps we shall not mention the manner of your arrival. Her mother – a most excellent sort of woman, but…"

"Not the sort of person who believes in magic?" said Ruby.

"Quite so. Quite so. Oh! Mrs Broderick! My dear Isabella!"

All the grown-ups and Camille stood up as two women came into the room. Alex and Ruby looked with interest at Isabella.

She was, Alex supposed, probably supposed to be pretty. (He was never quite sure how to tell, except possibly with film stars, who never looked like real people anyway.) She was dressed in an outfit that was somewhere between Eleanor's and the Countess's in terms of grandness: a long, loose dress decorated with little flowers. Unlike the

Countess, her hair was not powdered. Her mother was small and sharp-looking, with the sort of face that seemed to be looking out for something to frown at. At the sight of all the people in the drawing room, it twisted up on itself.

"Pray, excuse me, Mr Pilgrim," she said, rather coldly. "I was not aware that you were expecting guests."

"Ah! For that you must blame me," said the Countess. She dropped a deep curtsey in the woman's direction, and Camille bowed. Alex and Ruby quickly did the same. "I am Jeanne Darbonney, Countess d'Allonette, and this is my son, Camille Darbonney, Baron de Connett. We have escaped the sad state of affairs in France, and come to your village to put ourselves at the mercy of our old acquaintance, Mr Pilgrim."

"A countess!" The woman had gone pink. "Oh! My apologies, Lady Allonette, I was not aware, or naturally I would not have been so ill-mannered. Mr Pilgrim is a *dear* friend and guest of ours. He dines with us two or three times a month! You and Lord Connett must dine with us too – we insist upon it! Oakden is *quite* the only house in the area, I assure you."

Oakden! That was the big house in the village. Alex looked at Isabella with interest. Ruby, however, wasn't impressed.

"What about us?" she whispered indignantly to Alex.

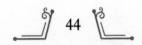

Frederick laughed.

"Do not worry, sweet cousins, you are not forgotten! These, my dear, are my young cousins, Ruby and Alex Pilgrim. They are come to stay while their mother is – ah – expecting a happy event at home." (Having a baby, Alex supposed this meant.) "Friends, may I present Mrs Broderick and her daughter, Miss Broderick, who has done me the very great honour of consenting to be my wife."

The men did a funny sort of half-bow, and the women curtsied. Alex and Ruby copied them as best they could.

Isabella looked at the Countess and – there was no other word for it – *simpered*.

"Oh!" she said. "Lady Allonette! My lady! Oh! What an honour! I am all delight! To have escaped the terrible, *terrible* situation in France! To be here, in my own Frederick's drawing room! Of course you must stay! Do not consider leaving! It must not be thought of!"

Alex glanced at the Countess. She was wearing a stiff, rather formal expression. He knew that face. It was the one Ruby used to make when their grandmother tried to tell her she was clever for winning the sort of certificate that was given to every child on Sports Day.

If she didn't like Isabella, however, she was far too polite to show it. She murmured, "You are most kind, Miss Broderick," and submitted to be simpered at for several minutes.

They all went and sat down on the chairs around the fireplace. More tea and cheese and cold meats were ordered – this time, however, they were delivered by a rather shabby-looking footman in a powdered wig and breeches with a hole in them.

A lot of boring grown-up conversation followed – mostly led by Isabella and her mother. Mrs Broderick evidently considered herself an important person in the village – she talked a lot about a ball she was planning on having at Christmas, about how many different courses she served at dinner, and how last year someone called Lady Maria had visited them and said nice things about the tableware.

"But a countess! Such an honour! And from France! Pray, you must tell me all about it. Have all your family been guillotined? Such a tragedy! Why, if Robespierre were here now, I would give him a piece of my mind!"

The Countess's face was perfectly blank, but Camille looked horrified. Even Frederick saw it, and quickly said, "Too horrible to talk of on such a pleasant day, is it not? Would you care for more tea, Lady Allonette?"

"And how came you to Dalton, Lady Allonette?" said Isabella. She'd been watching the Countess with a rather calculating expression. "Frederick never spoke of you before – I shall tease him about it most severely!"

"Mr Pilgrim is an old family friend," said the Countess. "And we have nowhere else to go. We are exceedingly grateful for his hospitality."

"Well!" Now Isabella very definitely looked put out. "Nowhere else to go, indeed! But – forgive me, my lady." She gave a tinkly little laugh. "You cannot expect to live here?"

There was a sharp intake of breath from Eleanor. But the Countess, by some miracle, kept her composure.

"As to that, who can say?" she said. "My brother Philippe is somewhere in the world – I know not where. My mother is in Russia. My friends may be dead, or else scattered to the winds. I will endeavour to discover their whereabouts, but…"

She spread her hands in a gesture of surrender. Isabella gave the same little laugh.

"Oh! How distressing it all is! But – forgive me my rudeness, my lady, but I must ask, since *dear* Frederick is to be my husband." A simper in Frederick's direction. "Your ladyship has property, I assume? Gold, jewels, money, smuggled out of France with which to support yourself?"

"Alas, no." The Countess's face was still astonishingly calm. "We have nothing. We come as we are. We throw ourselves entirely upon your Christian mercy."

"Oh!" Isabella and her mother exchanged a brief but meaningful look. "Oh! How comical!"

Ruby kicked Alex sharply on the ankle. He gave

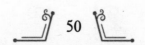

50

her a small nod back.

Neither of them needed to say any more.

This woman was trouble.

According to the clock on the drawing-room mantelpiece, it was now past three o'clock. They had been in Georgian Dalton since about eleven in the morning, and nobody had said anything about lunch. Surely Georgian people ate? That wasn't what those little cakes and slice of ham were supposed to be, was it?

He and Ruby wandered over to the table in the corner where the remains of the food were laid. Camille and Isabella were already there, filling their teacups with tea.

"Isn't it nearly lunchtime?" Ruby said.

"Lunchtime?" said Isabella. She frowned.

"She means luncheon," said Camille. There was definitely a look of mischief in his eyes as he said it, as though luncheon was a joke; though whether it was a joke on Ruby or Isabella, Alex wasn't sure.

Isabella bristled. "*Dinner*," she said frostily, "is at four o'clock. I hope you may wait until then. If you cannot, perhaps Cook can bring you up some

bread and butter with tea."

She turned stiffly, and went back over to the sofa where Frederick and the Countess were sitting. Ruby looked at Camille in bewilderment.

"What was all that about?"

"Luncheon is for peasants," said Camille briefly. "Those who get up with the dawn. Fashionable families eat late and rise late. Four is very early; in Versailles we take our dinner at seven, but then –"

and he looked disdainfully around at the beautiful drawing room –"this *is* the provinces."

Alex thought of their little red-brick house back home, with the handkerchief lawn-and-a-patio garden and not even one spare bedroom and never enough space in the cupboards. Alex's mum was a matron at their local hospital, and his dad worked for an antique dealer in town, restoring old furniture. Applecott House was lovely, of course, but just because Alex's grandfather had been born there, it didn't mean Alex would ever live anywhere like that.

What would Camille think if he could see their house? Would he care?

"It is to save on candlelight," said Eleanor

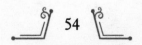

gently. "Candles are very dear, are they not? The later one eats, the more candles one must burn. Do you not have candles in the distant future?"

"Oh!" Alex supposed that made sense. "No, we've got, er, electric lights. You press a button and the light turns on."

"Gracious!" said Eleanor. "Our world must seem excessively dull, after living with such wonders."

"It's really not that exciting," said Ruby.

"Even the extraordinary becomes ordinary when it is all one knows," said Eleanor. Her eyes turned to the Countess, who was standing with Isabella and Frederick. Isabella, Alex saw, was still complaining about them.

"Really!" she said. "Frederick, my dear, what *are*

those children wearing? That child is indecent! Are they planning some sort of theatricals?"

"Indecent!" Ruby looked in confusion at her jeans and strappy top. "You should see what some of the kids in my year wear! These are practically nun clothes!"

There was a small noise from behind them. It was Eleanor, who was trying not to laugh.

"Come!" she said. "Miss Broderick is quite correct – it is not nice for a girl to go about in public in breeches, no matter her age." She smiled at Frederick and raised her voice. "Do you not have any more decent apparel, Mr Pilgrim?"

"Indeed I do!" Frederick beamed. "I have the very thing – a chest of clothing donated by the good people of my parish for the poor. If you would be so good as to assist me, ma'am?"

He bowed to Eleanor, who nodded her head in agreement.

"Come," she said, holding out her hand. "Let us see what we can make of you."

CHAPTER FOUR
THE TRUTH ABOUT
GEORGIAN UNDERWEAR

Frederick showed them into a small room on the first floor. Alex guessed it must be a spare bedroom of some sort. There was a low wooden bed under the window, and various chests and trunks spread across the floor. There were no curtains

– instead there were big wooden shutters, which Eleanor opened to let the light in. The room was already beginning to grow dark. There were no electric lights, of course, or even any firelight, and nobody had thought to give them a candle. (In the stately homes their parents liked to visit, there were always huge candelabras dangling from the ceiling, but it had never occurred to him to wonder how servants and poor people did things like cook their dinner or get dressed. How many candles would someone like Eleanor have in her room? He bet it wasn't a whole candelabra.)

Eleanor waited until they were in the room, then shut the door behind them.

"Oof!" she said, and sat down on the bed.

Alex laughed. "It is a bit much, isn't it?" he said.

"I own, I am all confusion," said Eleanor. "This morning I was in France, awaiting a gaol cell. And now I am here!"

"You get used to it," said Ruby. She thought about it. "Actually, no, you don't; it's always weird. It's good fun, though."

Eleanor laughed. "If two children can speak of it with such complacency, I dare say I shall too. Now, come! Let us find you something to wear."

Clothes in 1795 were properly dreadful.

They were given two full sets each – everyday clothes for daytime use, and a nicer set to wear in the evenings.

"I do not imagine Mr Pilgrim would expect you to dress for dinner if he were at home alone," Eleanor said. "But he will certainly do so while Isabella and the Countess are here."

Because it was nearly dinner time, they put on the fancier clothes first. Ruby had it worse – girls usually did, Alex was beginning to realise. First, she had a long cotton shift, sort of like an old-fashioned nightdress, which Eleanor called her chemise. Then there were stockings; these were made of wool and were hand-knitted. The stockings were followed by a real corset, which Eleanor called her "stays". It was made of whalebone, and had strings at the front and back that you pulled to tighten it. It was, Alex knew, supposed to squash up all your internal organs and give you a tiny waist.

"Oh, here we go," said Ruby, who had worn one before. But she submitted to being tightened. When the strings were tied, she walked cautiously across the room. "It changes the whole way you walk and stand. You have to stand perfectly straight," she explained, in answer to Alex's questioning look. "And it pushes your shoulders right back. It's *horrible*."

"I am sorry for it," said Eleanor. "But you must endeavour to endure it, if you wish to wear our clothes. And I fear you cannot wear those – those –" She gestured vaguely at where Ruby's knickers were underneath the shift.

"I don't see why not," Ruby grumbled. "It's not like anyone's going to see them."

"No, indeed!" Eleanor looked shocked. "But once you are in your chemise and your stays and your petticoats and your gown, then how will you – that is to say, when you need to visit… It will not be possible…" She blushed.

Alex said helpfully, "She means how will you take your knickers off to go to the loo when you're wearing all those skirts and things? She's got a point. You can barely bend down right now."

"But –" Ruby stared. "But you mean, wear *nothing*? No knickers!"

"To be sure," said Eleanor. "What! So surprised? It is natural, is it not?"

"Hmm," said Ruby. Victorian girls hadn't worn knickers either, but Ruby had kept hers on anyway. But Eleanor was right – this time, she didn't really have any choice about it.

Over the chemise went the petticoats, and over the petticoats went the gown, which even Alex thought was rather lovely. It was made of pale green muslin with little flowers on it, and had long loose skirts and slippers in pale green. Ruby, however, was unimpressed.

"These sleeves are *awful*," she said. "I can't move my arms properly." She demonstrated; her arms came a little way out from her body, then stopped. "It's like they're *designed* to make life as difficult as possible for you."

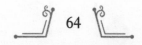

64

"Why, yes! It is very disagreeable, is it not? But see how it improves your deportment."

Deportment, Alex remembered from doing the Victorians at school, meant learning how to walk properly by balancing books on your head. He hoped boys' clothes weren't going to be so bad.

They were not. Georgian boys wore long shirts, which came somewhere down Alex's thighs. Over the shirt went a waistcoat – which Eleanor called a vest – and a topcoat with tails. They also wore white silk stockings, which came up to the knee and had to be kept in place with garters. To Alex's surprise, his silk stockings were threaded with darns, which made them rather painful to walk in. He hadn't known you could darn silk.

Over the stockings went breeches, which were like close-fitting knee-length shorts, only fancier. Posh shorts. And shoes with shiny brass buckles, which Alex thought looked utterly ridiculous (though not as ridiculous as the silk stockings).

Alex undressed with some embarrassment – he wanted to ask Eleanor to leave, but he wasn't sure he'd be able to manage the new clothes on his own. Eleanor looked away as much as she could, but the new clothes took some explaining, and she couldn't help but see his underpants.

"Oh!" she said. "You wear them too!"

"Yes…" Alex looked at her suspiciously. "You mean men here *don't*? But, I mean, doesn't it, well, doesn't it *rub*?"

Eleanor laughed, and blushed.

"You must use your shirt tails to – to…" She gestured vaguely.

Alex saw what she meant. He also saw that the breeches had buttons at the fly, meaning weeing was going to be a lot easier for him than it was for Ruby.

"Thanks," he said firmly. "But I think I'll leave mine on, if it's all the same to you."

"Lucky you," said Ruby. She looked helplessly at her skirts. "I don't know how I'm *ever* going to go to the loo in these," she said. "I think I'll just not bother eating or drinking anything ever again. Not that you *could* eat much in these stupid stays. And grown-ups think *modern* girls are obsessed with make-up and dieting."

"To be sure," said Eleanor. "'Tis most immodest for a young girl to care overmuch for her appearance. A girl may look very well without the fripperies of dress, may she not?"

Ruby stared. "You call all this living without the fripperies of dress?" she said. "Are you *insane*?"

After the clothes were on, Eleanor rang a bell and Helen appeared to direct them to their own room and then the toilet to finish their "ablutions". (This seemed to be a fancy old-fashioned word for doing a wee and having a wash.)

Their room was rather plain. There was no wardrobe; instead, they were given a large wooden chest to keep their clothes in. There were two beds, both incredibly uncomfortable; instead of springs, the mattresses were stuffed with goose feathers, and instead of slats, it rested on ropes criss-crossed beneath it. There was a little fireplace, but instead of a fire, there was an arrangement of pine cones in the grate. There was also a draught, and a damp spot on the wall above the bed.

Instead of curtains, the windows had shutters. They were small and diamond-paned, and looked out on to the back garden at Applecott House. This went on much further than Aunt Joanna's garden, and had a small woody bit in it, a big vegetable plot, and something that looked suspiciously like a chicken coop and a pig pen.

"Hey," said Ruby. "Do you think someone's going to come and curl my hair like Isabella's?"

"Nay," said Eleanor. "You are not fourteen. You are too young for such contrivances. But you must

both comb your hair and wash your hands and faces."

There was a basin and a jug full of warm water on a table by the window. Alex and Ruby did as they were told, and then Eleanor took them downstairs and to the toilet. This Applecott House didn't have a bathroom. Instead you used something called the "necessary house" (Eleanor, rather confusingly, called it "Jericho".). This was an actual wooden house in the back yard. It smelled disgusting, and, as Eleanor had prophesied, would have been almost impossible for Ruby to use with knickers on.

There was no water to wash your hands with and, instead of toilet paper, there were little sheets of torn-up newspaper hanging on a nail to wipe your bum on.

"Eugh!" said Ruby. "No wonder people in the past kept dying of cholera."

It made all the beauty feel decidedly less elegant. There was a water pump in the yard, and Alex and Ruby washed their hands, rather to the amusement of the servant girl.

"Now what?" said Ruby.

"Now dinner," said Eleanor. She pulled a face, then laughed. "*Courage!* Today, I escaped certain death. An English drawing room is as naught to that."

CHAPTER FIVE
AN UNSEEMLY AFFAIR

"Ah, there you are!" said Frederick, beaming, as they came down. "Capital, capital!"

He was still dressed all in black (it *must* be a vicar thing.) But the Countess wore a wonderfully elaborate silk dress, all embroidered with little pearls. Her hair and her make-up had been redone, and she looked – well, not beautiful exactly (Alex privately thought Eleanor in her plain grey dress looked much nicer) but very, very grand.

Isabella obviously thought so too. She was sending annoyed glances at the Countess, who was ignoring her and talking to Isabella's mother.

"Aye, in Versailles we would *never* dine before eight. But it is so quaint to observe these country customs. Mr Pilgrim's house is so charming! I declare myself quite delighted by it!"

"Indeed, indeed," Mrs Broderick murmured. "Eight, you say? Indeed. And, tell me, how were bonnets worn in Versailles this year?"

"Oh pish!" said Isabella. "Nobody cares about

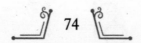

bonnets in Versailles, ma'am. They spend all their days guillotining their fellows!"

"'Tis true," said Frederick. He gave that same strange little bow to the Countess again. "And it is nothing to joke about. We are all very sorry for it, my lady."

"Indeed, we are!" said Mrs Broderick.

Isabella flushed. "Oh, well, as to that –" she said. "Naturally – I only meant–"

They were saved by the footman with his face powdered all over with what looked like white chalk, who appeared in the doorway, bowed, and said, "Dinner is served."

"At last!" said Ruby to Alex.

Dinner, despite it being four in the afternoon, was very fancy. Alex wasn't sure if it was in honour of the guests, or if Frederick ate like this every night. There was a soup course, a fish course, and a meat course, which was roast partridge – there was an actual bullet in Alex's portion, which Frederick called "shot". The vegetables, however, were rather strange; there was a sad-looking green mess on the corner of Alex's plate that turned out to be stewed cucumber. Alex felt like he'd been invited to a banquet or something – he kept wriggling in his seat and grinning at Ruby. Five courses! In fancy clothes! With a countess and a baron! Time travel didn't get much better than this.

It was wonderfully weird, and weirdly normal

at the same time. The fish was salmon, which tasted like ... well, like salmon from Tesco. The potatoes were potatoes and tasted like potatoes (though the butter was white instead of yellow). Alex had thought of things in the past as being completely different – all black-and-white and stiff, and ancient, and it was disorientating to find that some things were just the same as in the present.

The food was served by the footman, who stood behind each diner and spooned out the food on to their plates, making the whole thing feel very posh indeed. The posh feel was somewhat ruined by there being only one of him – Frederick evidently wasn't used to having five extra guests

turn up unexpectedly for dinner. He was helped
by the little servant girl, Helen, to the disapproval
of Isabella and Mrs Broderick.

"Good gracious, child!" Isabella said, as Helen
dropped sauce in her lap. "Are you a simpleton?
This gown is not a week old – you have ruined it,
I declare!"

"I am very sorry for it," Helen stammered. "I
did not mean—"

"It's only a bit of gravy!" said Ruby indignantly. "You can hardly see it! Don't be rude!"

"I? Rude?" Isabella drew herself up in a fury. "I wonder that your relations allow you to speak to your elders in such a manner!" She shot a furious look at Frederick.

"I am entirely to blame," he said quickly. "Helen is but a child, not used to waiting at table. Had I known there were to be so many for dinner,

naturally I would have made other arrangements."

"We are very grateful," said Eleanor quickly. "We had no right to expect anything at all."

Isabella subsided, muttering. There was a rather awkward pause, then: "As to that," she said suddenly, "my fiancé is the kindest man alive. I declare he will bankrupt himself if he continues like this!"

Ruby caught Alex's eye and gave her a meaningful look. Alex nodded. If Camille and the Countess were going to stay here, they would have to do something about Isabella.

"More wine, ma'am?" said the footman quickly.

All the grown-ups were drinking wine. The children had ale. Alex looked at his a bit dubiously.

"Won't we get drunk?" he whispered to Camille.

Camille shook his head. "Nay," he said. "'Tis only weak stuff."

Alex took a cautious sip. It tasted absolutely disgusting, even worse than the tea.

"Eugh! Isn't there any water?"

"They didn't drink water in the olden days," Ruby said. "We did it in school. Because they didn't have water purification or anything, so it made them sick. I expect it would make us *doubly* sick, because we don't have immunity, like when the American settlers gave all the Native Americans smallpox or something. We'd better drink it, I reckon."

This aspect of time travel had not occurred to

Alex, despite his previous adventures. Were he and Ruby going to catch cholera or scarlet fever or something dreadfully old-fashioned like that? Just to be on the safe side, he thought he'd better drink the ale. Camille was evidently right, because he didn't feel much different afterwards. Only rather full and sleepy.

It was beginning to grow dark, and the footman came in carrying candles on big multi-candle candlesticks. This was rather lovely, and gave a strange, warm, dim yellow glow to the room. The candles had long wicks that trailed down the sides of the candles when they grew too long, and had to be cut by Helen with a pair of special scissors. Alex wriggled again. Dinner by candlelight! Over two hundred years ago!

"This is *brilliant*!" he whispered to Ruby, and she gave a cautious smile.

"It isn't so bad, I suppose," she admitted.

There was no pudding, just a plate with different sorts of cheeses, and another with raisins and figs and dates. After they'd finished eating, the women and children went into the drawing room, leaving Frederick to drink a glass of port and smoke his cigar. Isabella and her mother immediately went into the corner to whisper to themselves – their whole demeanour was so obviously exclusive that none of the others would have approached them, even if they wanted to.

Which they didn't.

"Isabella is *awful*," said Ruby, as soon as the door had closed behind the footman. "Why on *earth* is Frederick marrying her? She's horrible!"

"She is a handsome woman," said the Countess with a grim smile. "Many a wiser man than Mr Pilgrim has married for less."

"Well, men are idiots!" said Ruby.

The Countess inclined her head. "Naturally so."

"Look here," said Alex. "Do we want Frederick to marry Isabella? I mean, if we're supposed to be finding you a home, you *can't* live here with her, can you? It would be horrible."

"For all concerned," murmured Camille.

Alex shot a look at him, and he grinned and waggled his eyebrows.

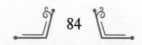

"Miss Broderick is an ignorant, foolish child," said the Countess. "I would not live in her house for a thousand pounds. But I doubt I will be given the chance. Though her snobbery may be flattered by the idea of playing hostess to a countess, I fear her good opinion of herself would never tolerate the reminder of her own inferiority."

"But where are you going to go?" said Alex practically. "Do you know *anyone* in Britain?"

"I have commanded Mr Pilgrim to write to his bishop. He tells me there are organisations devoted to the support of royalist refugees. But beyond that..."

She spread her arms in a gesture of futility.

"*Can't* you get a job?" Ruby said.

"Doing what?" said Eleanor. "A woman may not join the army, or practise the law. She may not join the church or attend the university. She cannot run away to sea. A woman of noble birth may be a governess or a lady companion, but one requires a certain temperament to do either, and I fear my ladyship would fare very poorly."

"And there's Camille as well, I suppose," said Alex.

"Oh! Do not concern yourself with me," said Camille grandly. "I'm for the army. Together, we shall fight the usurpers of our nation, and ride victorious into Paris!"

"Unless you join as a drummer boy, you will need money to buy your commission," said

Eleanor. "Your lady mother has none, nor does Mr Pilgrim."

"Oh! I do not mind that," said Camille. "I would rather serve as a pot washer than go begging."

He looked very noble as he said it, but Alex couldn't help but wonder if he'd ever actually *washed* a pot.

"Look," said Ruby, "whenever the mirror takes us somewhere, it's because there's a problem we need to help solve. And you guys *don't* have a home, so, like Eleanor said, that's obviously what we have to do. We can't find your relatives for you, but we *can* get rid of Isabella. Well, we can try. So I think we should do that for now, and see if anything else comes up. I mean, Frederick's lovely, and she's awful. He's going to be miserable if he marries her, so even if you don't end up living here, splitting them up is a good idea anyway. Don't you think?"

The Countess gave Ruby a long, appraising look.

"I think you are a very direct young lady," she said. "Are all women in your time so forthright?"

"No," said Alex. "I mean, yeah, a bit, but Ruby's the noisiest. She's got a point, though, hasn't she? Surely Frederick would be happier if he dumped her?"

"It would be most ungentlemanly for Mr Pilgrim to break the engagement," said Countess. "He would not do it, I lay. But I agree that if Isabella were to end it, it would be the better for him."

"My lady!" Eleanor looked distressed. "Mr Pilgrim and Miss Broderick are not children. It is not our place to decide if they should be wed or not."

"Oh, pish!" said the Countess. "Mr Pilgrim is – what? – two-and-twenty? He is barely breached!"

"Well, I shall not be a part of it," said Eleanor. "I think it is most unseemly behaviour and—"

But the door behind her was opening.

"What ho!" cried Frederick.

And the conversation was done.

The rest of the evening was surprisingly good fun. They played a card game called "lottery tickets";

you had to put little tokens on the cards, and if you were dealt a card that matched one on the table, you won all the tokens. The children seemed to be considered honorary grown-ups, and were allowed to join in instead of being sent off upstairs, as they would have been at one of Aunt Joanna's family parties. The yellow candlelight and the fire in the grate gave the whole thing a rather thrilling air, like being at the theatre or telling ghost stories in the dark. The candles gave out far less light in real life than in the period dramas Alex's parents watched. There was a largish candelabra in the centre of the room, and other candles set in sconces on the walls. They gave out a warm, quavering orange light, much softer and somehow *alive* in a way that electric light wasn't. When the door opened, the flames shivered and the shadows leaped against the wall. It was a little bit spooky and a little bit comforting, all at once.

As the evening wore on, Alex and Ruby found themselves growing sleepier and sleepier. Didn't children have bedtimes in Georgian times? If so, they must be very late. It was long past Alex's usual bedtime when Eleanor noticed him drooping in the chair and sent them to bed.

Going to bed was fun, though rather spooky. There were no lights in the hall or the corridor at all; each child was given a single candle in a Wee-Willie-Winkie-style holder, and that was expected to be enough. It was, just, though it was rather dim, and left mysterious shadows in the corner of the bedroom. Alex was very pleased that Ruby and Eleanor were there. They were expected to wash before bed, with the washstand and the jug, and use the chamberpot. Teeth were cleaned with tooth powder, and a toothbrush with bristles made out of actual pig hair.

"Pig hair!" said Ruby.

The tooth powder tasted of cloves and left a weird aftertaste. Ruby spat it out and refused to even try it again.

"I'd rather all my teeth fell out!" she said.

"That very thing happened to my uncle," said Eleanor cheerfully. "He has a set of battlefield teeth – from corpses, you know," she added, seeing their puzzlement.

"Your uncle has teeth taken from *dead bodies*?" said Ruby. Her expression was so appalled that Alex had to laugh. So did Eleanor.

"Why, yes," she said. "My lady has eyebrows made from mouse skin too," she added teasingly.

"Mouse eyebrows!" Ruby stared. "God, I'm *so glad* I live in the twenty-first century."

There were no pyjamas, or even nightgowns. Alex was to sleep in his shirt and Ruby her shift, though they were given funny cloth nightcaps with pointed tips to keep the cold out. It was very cold, even in bed, even with the piles of blankets and the eiderdown. The whole room was cold;

there was no fire, nor any central heating, of course. Victorian England had been just the same. And when Alex blew out the candle, it was very, very dark. No street lights. No car lights passing underneath the window. Just blackness. Alex had never got used to this part of being in the past.

He curled up into a ball and tried to pretend that he didn't mind, but it was a very long time indeed before he was warm enough to sleep.

CHAPTER SIX
A PLOT IS HATCHED

Alex woke late the next morning to the sound of Helen bringing a jug of warm water into the bedroom.

"Hello," he said curiously. He was a little shy of her – she was about Ruby's age or a bit older, and he didn't think she'd want to make friends with a kid like him. She bobbed an awkward sort of curtsey.

"Good morning, Master Pilgrim," she said, and ducked under the bed for the chamberpot. Alex looked away in embarrassment, and then she was gone.

Breakfast didn't start until ten. It was not eaten in the dining room, but in Frederick's study.

"'Tis just toast and chocolate, nothing more," Helen said, which sounded hopeful. Alex liked the sound of chocolate for breakfast.

This turned out not to mean bars of chocolate, but cocoa, with rough-looking lumps of sugar to drop into it. The bread was toasted on the end of a long fork on the study fire. Camille and Alex and Ruby did most of the toasting, which was surprisingly good fun, only it took rather a long time to toast enough bread for them all.

After breakfast, Eleanor went quietly up to Frederick.

"Think you we could walk into the village this morning?" she said. "There are certain – sundries – my lady greatly desires, and she would be much relieved if they could be purchased."

She didn't say what exactly the Countess wanted, but Alex supposed she meant the Georgian equivalent of toothbrushes and hairbrushes and clean knickers. New mouse eyebrows, perhaps.

Frederick seemed to understand.

"But naturally!" he said. "Perhaps you might permit me to escort you? Would the children care to come too?"

Camille gave a very French, one-sided shrug.

"It does not concern me," he said. (Which Alex supposed meant "OK").

"Well, *I'd* like to come," said Ruby.

Frederick, meanwhile, had hunted through a pile of ancient newspapers, all (of course) without photographs, and written up in tiny type. Hidden amongst the news, he'd found advertisements for several charitable organisations dealing with the concerns of French refugees. They left the

Countess with an inkpot and a quill pen, writing letters to these good people, and set off.

Alex and Ruby were used to the strangeness of pre-tarmac roads. They were either horribly dusty, or horribly muddy, with enormous great clags of mud that stuck to your boots, depending on the rain. It had evidently been quite dry recently, because this road was all dust. It was also a mess of potholes, cart tracks, and grass. Camille stumped along beside them, his face set in a frown.

"Do you not have a carriage?" he said sourly.

"Indeed I do," said Frederick cheerfully. "But not one that would take five, alas. Besides, it is not a mile to the village, and 'tis a pleasant walk on a fine day."

But Camille's scowl deepened.

"Why," he said to Eleanor, "if you are a witch and could take us anywhere, do you choose to send us *here*?"

"I *told* you," said Ruby. "The mirror can only take you to places where it's been. You go into *that* mirror and come out into the same mirror twenty years ago, or two hundred, or into the future or whatever."

"But she is a witch," Camille said. "She sets the laws of this magic, does she not?"

"I know not," said Eleanor. She spread out her arms. "Would that I did! I believe I am controlled by it." Her face darkened. "Indeed, if I could be rid of it, I would."

"Oh, don't!" said Alex. He spoke with more vehemence than he'd intended, and the others looked at him with surprise. "It's just – well. The mirror is kind – I know it is. I don't know if it's because, well, because you made it, and you're kind too. Or if it's the magic that's good. But it always seems to want things that are – well, worth having, you know. If it's brought us here, it'll have a good reason, I promise."

"Upon my word!" cried Frederick. "I'll lay the young gentleman is right! Why! A girl with such good sense as Eleanor – she could cast no wicked spell, I am certain of it. Her looking glass will be as sweet and amiable as she is herself. I can picture it now, sending us to the general store to buy sundries, tending to the little sorrows of those around it."

"Would that it was so!" said Eleanor. "My magic is many things, but considerate it is not. Why! It did not even permit me to pack a change of linen!"

"A mere trifle," said Frederick. "It has temporarily mislaid its manners, I am sure. When we return, we shall find all your possessions, delivered by magical winds across the sea, with clean stockings and freshly laundered handkerchiefs for all!"

He took her arm in a companionable fashion. She laughed. So did Alex.

Camille was looking at them both with unconcealed amazement.

"Upon my soul," he said. "You are as much a jackanapes as she!"

They walked along the path in companionable silence for a while. Alex looked around. He still couldn't get used to how the countryside in the past was both the same and different. Trees and clouds and walls just looked like trees and clouds and walls. But in so many other ways, the countryside was different. They passed one farm where the harvest was clearly in progress; the field was full of men, women and children with scythes and baskets full of wheat. Alex thought it looked quite fun, everyone working together, but he couldn't help but notice how small some of the children were. Didn't they go to school? In another field, a little boy who looked about seven had been left all alone to scare the birds. He was running up and down the field, waving his hands and shouting. His feet were bare, despite the cold, and he stopped as they passed and stared at them with unabashed curiosity. *What a job!* Alex thought. Did he do that all day, on his own? Was that *normal*?

As usual, the countryside was wilder, less tamed – there was a profusion of flowers shooting up amongst the corn and on the verges, and birds in the trees, and wild grass amongst the potholes. It even smelled different, richer and thicker and earthier. They passed a meadow full of wild flowers and the scent was dizzying. Like breathing in honey.

Ruby, as usual, wasn't paying any attention to her surroundings. She gave Alex a meaningful look and jerked her head at Frederick. Alex gave a half-shrug that was supposed to say "Go on then, if you want to". He didn't have the first idea how you were supposed to even *start* breaking two people up.

But Ruby didn't seem to know either. She walked along for a bit, looking awkward, then said, "So … Isabella. Have you, er, known her long?"

"Indeed no!" said Frederick enthusiastically. "I have not been three months in this parsonage. But there! It takes a mere moment to fall in love, does it not?"

"Dunno," said Ruby. "I'm thirteen. Er, what attracted you to her?"

"What did not?" Frederick said dreamily. "Her eyes … her figure… She is uncommonly pretty, is she not?"

Alex and Ruby looked at each other.

"She's all right," said Alex.

"She does not compare to the beauties of Versailles," said Camille, in a lordly tone.

"She's a bit … overdone, isn't she?" said Ruby. "I mean, all those curls and so forth."

"'Tis the fashion," said Eleanor quickly.

But Frederick laughed. "Well! She is more handsome than a ragtag parson like myself should ever dream to entangle."

"Yeah, why *does* she like you?" said Ruby.

"Ruby!" said Alex, horrified.

"What? It's a perfectly reasonable question! He's not that handsome. He hasn't got any money. She's *totally* the sort of girl who'd want to marry a duke or something. I mean, no offence," she said quickly, though Frederick looked more amused than offended. "You're very nice. But, well—"

"'Tis a good match for a ragamuffin like myself? Indeed it is. And, indeed, I did not expect that she would ever consider my suit. But there, I was lucky. Her parents had intended that she should marry a man of fifty-five. Naturally, to a young girl like Isabella, that thought was not pleasing.

So when I pressed my suit, she was minded to look upon it more favourably and the gentleman was obliged to form an alliance with another lady. Am I not the most fortunate man alive?"

"Hmm," said Ruby.

Alex agreed. This story didn't exactly sound like the Romance of the Century.

"Seriously, though," she said. "You can't marry someone just because they look pretty. What about... I dunno. Shared interests? Hobbies?"

"Oh, pish! She can tinkle a pretty tune at the piano, and I dare say she can sew a cunning screen. It does not signify how a woman entertains herself."

"On the contrary, sir." Despite herself, Eleanor

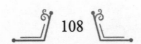

had entered the debate. "A husband and wife must perforce be very much together. Without a commonality of interest and understanding, their married life must be a misery. Our religion teaches that marriage should not be entered into lightly – as a man of God, you must be mindful of that."

She spoke with a vehemence that surprised Alex, and evidently Frederick too.

"Well, well!" he said. He shook his head. Then: "I dare say you are right. But Isabella is a very sweet girl, you know, a very sweet girl indeed."

"Naturally," said Eleanor drily.

They passed the rest of the walk in silence.

Modern Dalton was quite a large village. In 1795,

it was much, much smaller. The only buildings Alex could recognise were the church, the pub, which was almost unrecognisable, and *perhaps* one or two of the houses, *maybe*, with different doors and windows and roofs, and all the extensions and garden walls and television aerials gone.

What remained was a little cluster of houses, grouped around the green (which was larger and wilder-looking than the modern green, and had actual cows on it), a small, old-fashioned grocer's shop, a baker's, a blacksmith's, and a shop selling what looked like cloth. The roads were dirt tracks and mostly empty, apart from some chickens, a couple of small boys playing by the edge of the duck pond and a dog, dozing by the pub door.

There was also a windmill.

"A windmill!" Alex said, delighted.

"Why, yes," said Frederick. "How else would one grind corn?"

"Indeed," said Eleanor. "Every village must have a windmill, must it not?"

"I suppose so," said Alex. It was all rather disorientating.

They walked around the village. Eleanor stopped at several shops – the dressmaker's and the general store – and Frederick seemed to stop every five minutes to say "Good morning!" to somebody else and introduce them. He seemed to know absolutely everyone who lived there. Alex supposed he would, being the vicar.

After all Eleanor's commissions were filled, Frederick gave the children a small bag of what he called "sugar plums", but which turned out to be nuts covered in sugar, like the sugared almonds they sometimes had at Christmas. Then they all went over to the blacksmith's to talk about some problem with his horse. This was a fascinating world of fire and sparks and metal, and they spent some time watching the smith and his boy at work. But once this was over, the men all began a long, complicated horsey conversation. Eleanor, Alex and Ruby soon grew bored, and went to sit in the long grass, eat sugar plums, and wait.

"May I ask you a question?" said Eleanor. "The bottle that you say Alex found – the one he opened and wished upon before you first travelled through my lady's looking glass – what was it like?"

Alex tried to remember. "It was quite small – about this big." He held his hands apart to demonstrate. "It was made of silver, and it had flowers and things on it, I think. There was a cork stopper at the top."

"Like this?" Eleanor had a small leather pouch hanging from her belt – like a sort of purse. She opened it, and took out…

"That's it!" Alex cried. "That's the bottle! I mean, it looks newer than our bottle –" Aunt Joanna's witch in a bottle had been rather dented and tarnished – "but it's definitely the same one! Where did you get it? Is it a special potion bottle or something?"

"Nay!" Eleanor shook her head. "'Tis for scent." She held up the bottle to the light, her head on one side. "Would that there *were* a witch imprisoned inside who could grant our wishes! Our futures are tossed on the seas of time, and we must trust that your looking glass guides us safely to the shore."

It was an odd way of putting it, Alex thought, but rather a nice one. He smiled at Eleanor. She, however, was looking over his shoulder. An odd, rather stiff expression had appeared on her face.

"What?" said Ruby, and turned to look.

It was Isabella.

CHAPTER SEVEN
CHIT-CHAT AND GOVERNESSES

Exclamations of delight. The usual English chit-chat about the weather. Frederick was clearly in high spirits.

"What a delightful coincidence to see you here!" he said joyfully.

"Why, yes!" said Isabella, but she sounded rather distracted. She was eyeing up Camille and Eleanor behind her fan.

"We have just been making some purchases for the Countess – so difficult when one has come all the way from France, is it not?"

"Oh! You are doing her shopping now, are you? How quaint! Quite the devoted admirer, Frederick – you will make me quite jealous! How is the darling Countess? So exciting to have a fugitive from justice staying in one's parsonage! Does not the bishop object?"

"Object! Why, Isabella, do not be absurd. Toppling the pretenders in France is the dearest wish of our redcoats, is it not? Camille and the

Countess will be celebrated in the streets!"

"My dear!" Isabella simpered. "I hardly think it likely, in Dalton! But tell me, I beg you. How does she intend to support herself? Does she sing, write, dance? Can she teach? She must know that on a parson's salary, you cannot be expected to pay for her lady's maid, and folderols."

"She doesn't have a maid," said Ruby. "Er, does she?" She looked at Alex uncertainly. Alex thought of the corset, with all its string, and the Countess's elaborately natural ringlets. Helen had, he knew, been in to lace up Ruby that morning. Had she been maiding for the Countess too? It didn't seem likely.

"No maid!" said Isabella. "Nay, Frederick, it is

hopeless to deceive a lady on such matters! How many servants did she bring with her?"

Frederick looked uncomfortable.

Eleanor said in her calm voice, "Her ladyship brought no maid. I have been maiding for her since we came to England."

It was brief but Alex saw it – a flash of triumph in Isabella's eyes.

"You! Maiding! My dear! Such humiliation! I could not bear it, were it I!"

Eleanor's face did not change, but Ruby's darkened.

"It's not Eleanor's fault the Countess doesn't have a maid!" she said. "She was escaping the soldiers of the revolution! At least Eleanor *does*

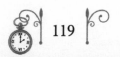

something! She doesn't just sit there expecting everyone to wait on her like *some* people I could mention!"

"Oh! How can you say such a thing!"

"Ruby!" said Eleanor. "Pray be silent! It is most indecorous for a girl your age to speak so! You must apologise at once."

"Oh, pish!" cried Frederick. Isabella glared at him. "Bravo, say I! I am sure my lady meant no ill by her words – she is all sweetness! – but Ruby is quite right. It is a noble thing to fend for oneself in a man's world, and we must not twit Eleanor for it. Tell me, how old were you when you first became a governess?"

"I was not seventeen," said Eleanor. Alex

supposed that meant she was sixteen, though it seemed an odd way of saying it. "Perhaps it *was* full young to be so independent. But after the death of my parents, it was that or marry, and I did not choose to marry against the inclination of my heart."

"Well, of course not!" said Ruby. "I would hate that too. But do you actually like being a governess? Wouldn't you rather do something else instead?"

"I would, indeed. But, pray, what would you have me do? The world is not kind to a woman making her own way in the world."

"I suppose not." Ruby was quiet.

Beside her, Isabella made an irritated sort of noise.

"I am excessively glad that *I* need never work for my living," she said. "Why! I could imagine nothing worse than being a governess. Living in a stranger's house, teaching arithmetic to pratting infants." She gave a rather feminine shudder.

Camille shot her a look of distaste.

"I think it's brilliant," said Alex.

"You are very kind," said Eleanor. "But your compliments are misplaced. I had little choice in the matter."

"Aye," said Frederick. "But to go to Versailles, at the height of the revolution!"

"Too dangerous for a woman, you mean? Perhaps. But I confess, a drawing-room sort of life does not suit me. I may be a woman, but I long for adventure."

"Now on that we are in agreement!" Frederick looked delighted. "What could be more dull? I too am a restless fellow. When I am at home, I *long* to be away."

"What unfortunate tastes for a clergyman!" said Isabella sourly. "Would not the army or the navy have better suited your purpose?"

"Indeed they would," said Frederick. "But, alas! My father would not support such an idea. I had always intended to join the navy, and go to sea as chaplain. Oh! I would like beyond anything to see New South Wales, and Africa, and the Americas."

"Oh, yes!" said Eleanor. Her face was shining. "Oh! How marvellous it would be!"

"Well, perhaps I shall go yet." He turned to Isabella, his face still alive with the joy of the idea. "Would not you like a shawl from the East Indies to wear on your pretty shoulders?"

"Indeed no!" She pulled a face. "I do not wish to be left behind in England while my husband is heaven-knows-where. Insupportable idea!"

"Then it is not be thought of," said Frederick grandly, kissing her hand. "I would rather give up all the Indies – north, south, east and west – than cause you a moment's sorrow."

"My dear!" *Now* Isabella looked pleased. As Frederick bent down to kiss her, she shot Eleanor a look of what can only be described as triumph.

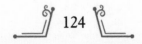

The rest of the day was quiet and uneventful. They went back to Applecott House and Frederick disappeared into his study. Eleanor took the children into an upstairs bedroom for "lessons", which consisted of her reading aloud from a dull history of the Roman Empire, and then letting them do a jigsaw puzzle of all the

different countries of the world, which they'd found in a drawer. This was rather difficult, as the writing was swirly and hard to read, and half of the countries had different names.

"Think you *Maman*'s letters will bear fruit?" asked Camille rather listlessly.

"I know not," said Eleanor. "But we must try not to be downhearted. Why! Think how narrowly we avoided a cell in the Bastille!"

Camille grunted. "*Maman* is writing to my *grandmère* in Russia," he said. "Perhaps she knows what has become of my Uncle Philippe and my Aunt Celeste. Uncle Philippe is a capital fellow; I do hope he survived."

"Perhaps we shall go to Russia," said Eleanor.

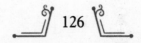

Her hands traced lightly over the map of the world. "That would be an adventure, would it not?"

Camille didn't look convinced.

"Only if one happens to like snow and samovars," he said. "Which I do not." He gave a huge sigh. Alex wondered what a samovar was. He had a vague idea it was a sort of Indian pasty. "But," Camille went on, "I suppose we must hope for something. For one thing is clear. If Mr Pilgrim marries Miss Broderick, we shall not be allowed to stay here."

Camille seemed to be right. The next day, Isabella "called upon" the family again. It was another disaster. She spent the whole visit making pointed remarks.

"When this is *my* house, we must have brother Sam to stay, you know. And the children. You could not expect me to live in a house without a guest bedroom, *could* you, darling? It would be insurmountable!"

Frederick smiled at her. "Ah, well, you know, my dear, a parson's house must always have an open door to strangers…"

"Indeed! It says so in the Bible, does it? How curious! I'm sure our old parson never said any such thing. And what of our children? I simply long to have children! And children must have nurseries, you know, and nursery maids."

"You know we're all sitting *right here?*" said Ruby loudly.

"Ruby!" said Eleanor.

Isabella gave Ruby a look. "When I was a child," she said pointedly to Frederick, "I knew better than to disrespect my elders. If I were you, I would reprimand that governess most severely. I don't know what she thinks she is about, to let a child speak like that in public!"

"She's not even my governess!" said Ruby. Eleanor shot her a look, and she quelled, contenting herself with muttering, "Well, you aren't."

"It is naturally very upsetting for the children," said Frederick, in a placating sort of voice.

"But I am afraid I could never reprimand Miss Crouchman. She is quite a remarkable sort of young woman. I doubt I could even bring myself to raise my voice to her."

He looked laughingly across at Eleanor, and though his tone was teasing, there was something in her face that caught his attention. The laughter died, and he seemed to stare. For a moment, Eleanor was similarly caught, then she looked away and said briskly to Ruby, "Miss Broderick is quite right, Ruby. Rudeness is never acceptable, no matter the provocation."

Ouch. Isabella flushed and looked from Eleanor to Frederick. Eleanor pushed her needle through Camille's glove, and pulled it out with a long, unconcerned sweep of her arm. Frederick seemed to be trying not to laugh.

Isabella looked furious.

Over the next couple of days, they began to fall into a sort of routine: after breakfast, the Countess wrote letters and read the English newspapers, and sat in the drawing room, taking calls from the neighbourhood. Quite a lot of the local gentry wanted to see her – Mrs Broderick and Isabella came most days, but so did people from various big houses in the area, and some quite small ones. They all wanted to talk about France, and how dreadful the situation was over there, and, *Oh, how abominable it all was* and *However had her*

ladyship escaped? and on and on. Lots of them left visiting cards, and Eleanor explained that now the Countess had to call on them in return.

"Why?" said Alex.

"So they can make friends, of course," said Ruby. "It sounds like a good idea to me. It's awful when you move somewhere and don't know anyone – it happened to my friend Iffath, they moved at the start of the summer holidays and the only people they knew were Iffath's cousins, who were awful, Iffath said, and she had to spend the whole summer hanging out with them. The Countess doesn't even have to bother joining an orchestra or anything like Iffath did; they all just arrive on the doorstep."

"But then she has to go and visit *them*," said Alex. Imagine knocking on a stranger's door, then having to go and sit in their drawing room and *talk* to them! The very idea made his insides curl up with horror. But Ruby looked at him like he was crazy.

"Of course she does!" she said. "How else is she going to make friends?"

While the Countess was doing this, Frederick was busy vicaring, which mostly seemed to mean visiting people.

"Don't you have to write sermons?" said Alex, but Frederick waved his hand.

"I have a book of them in my study," he whispered. "But hush! 'Tis a secret!"

The children continued to do lessons with Eleanor. Eleanor took this very seriously. Camille was expected to do Latin and Greek translations from the books in Frederick's study.

"But why?" said Ruby, and Camille said, "Every gentleman should know the classics," which didn't help much.

"What about every lady?" said Ruby, and Eleanor laughed.

"My father was an uncommonly learned gentleman, who determined that I should learn all that a boy would. But many young ladies have no schooling at all, you know. They are taught to read and write by their mothers, and to sew, and to sing, and play the piano. There *are* schools for girls, but I would not send a daughter of mine there. Girls learn to paint and to make tapestries, and little else I fear. How are girls educated in the future?"

"Just the same as boys!" said Ruby. "Me and Alex go to the same school – at least, we will next year. And we don't learn needlework and piano and Latin. We do Biology and Chemistry and Maths and – well, useful stuff."

"Pish!" said Camille. "There is more daily use to needlework than to mathematics."

"He's got a point," said Alex, grinning at Ruby.

"So why don't boys learn it then?" she demanded.

Eleanor laughed again. "An excellent riposte!"

she said. And for the rest of the lesson, they all had to learn how to make buttonholes. Camille and Ruby grumbled, but Alex rather enjoyed it. It was more interesting than the Roman Empire, at any rate.

CHAPTER EIGHT
DISASTER ON A
STAIRCASE

After their lessons, they had fruit and ale in the
schoolroom. Ruby was wrong about people always
drinking alcohol, though – there'd been wine at
dinner, but Eleanor had diluted hers with water,
and she'd had a glass of water as well. And of

course there was tea and chocolate too.

After the fruit, they were free to entertain themselves while the Countess and Frederick went to "pay calls", or to visit with Isabella. Frederick had a horse and carriage, with space for the driver and a single passenger. He didn't seem to have a coachman; he drove himself. When the carriage wasn't out, Camille was allowed to go riding on the horse. Alex would have loved a go too, but this was never suggested.

Eleanor was not invited on these trips; she stayed at home sewing. The Countess had turned up her nose at all the clothes in the "poor box", so Eleanor was busy making her a second dress. Since sewing machines hadn't been invented yet, she had to do the whole thing by hand.

"From *scratch*?" said Ruby.

"And very cunning it shall look too!" said Frederick.

Frederick was kept very busy attending to Isabella and the Countess, but he always stopped when he saw Eleanor, and sat beside her, and asked how she did.

"You look weary," he said one evening, as she sat yawning over the bodice. Isabella was giving a long lecture to the others on the barbarity of the French Revolution, and the French as a nation in general.

"A little perhaps," said Eleanor.

"Your mistress works you too hard," he said,

suddenly angry. "It is not your place to be her governess, her maid *and* her seamstress."

"I do not mind it," said Eleanor, but she did look tired.

Frederick seemed to tense. "It is not your place," he repeated. He got up and left the room abruptly. The children looked at each other.

"What was that about?" said Ruby.

Eleanor bent her head over her stitching. She did not answer.

"Mr Pilgrim is a fine gentleman," said Camille. He was watching Eleanor. She seemed to gather herself together.

"Yes," she said. "Very fine." But she did not look up.

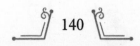

The door banged behind them. It was Frederick. He stood over Eleanor, watching her sew. He was still breathing heavily.

"I have spoken with Benjamin," he said. Benjamin was the footman. "His wife will be happy to finish her ladyship's gown for you."

"That is most kind of you, sir," said Eleanor. She did not look up. "But we have so little money. Her ladyship could not afford—"

"I shall pay," said Frederick. "I insist."

Eleanor's needle paused. She still did not look up.

"Her ladyship will be most grateful," she said.

"Her ladyship be damned!" Now Eleanor did look up, and her face was scarlet. "I did not do it for her ladyship, dash it," said Frederick. "I did it for you."

Alex looked quickly at Isabella. Her face had darkened with anger. She cast a quick glance at Frederick and Eleanor, then back at the others.

"I don't care who you are," she hissed at the Countess in fury. "Or who that impudent strumpet thinks she is. But I tell you now: I shall have you thrown out of this house and on to the streets, if it's the last thing I do."

The Countess did not bother to reply. But Alex and Ruby exchanged worried looks. She meant it. Alex was certain she did.

The children convened in the schoolroom.

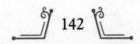

"He is in love with Eleanor," said Camille.

"He's engaged," said Alex. "And he's only known her a couple of days!" His parents had been together for three years before *they'd* got engaged.

"Nevertheless."

"Is she in love with him, though?" said Ruby practically.

They considered this. Eleanor was so quiet and reserved it was hard to tell what she was thinking.

"She *likes* him," said Alex.

"She is too honourable a lady to flirt with a gentleman who is engaged," said Camille. "But it would be a good match, I think. A clergyman is a very respectable sort of husband for a governess."

"I think they'd be lovely together," said Alex.

"I don't think Isabella even *likes* Frederick much. I bet she only got engaged to avoid marrying that other bloke. He'd be way happier with Eleanor."

"*Naturellement.*" Camille dismissed Isabella with a wave of his hand. "But what do we do now?"

"We watch them," said Ruby. "And we find out what they really think of each other. And then we … help them along. But we need to do it fast. Isabella won't let us stay here much longer."

"Helping them along" turned out to be very frustrating. When Isabella was there – which was often – she demanded all of Frederick's attention. When she was not, the Countess expected him to pay court to her. Eleanor sat neatly and quietly on the edge of the room with a book or some sewing, and watched them.

After a day of observing, they compared notes.

1.   Eleanor offered to help Frederick sort out his hymn books, which were beginning to go mouldy. When he thanked her, she said she was only doing it because she was grateful for "all his kindness".

2.   On a walk into Dalton, Frederick walked with Eleanor the whole way and argued with her about people in the Bible. They seemed to disagree with everything the other one said, but they were both very excited about it and seemed to be enjoying themselves.

3.   The local doctor and his wife called on

Frederick, and spent the whole visit talking to the Countess and ignoring Eleanor, who sat quietly in her corner with her sewing. After about an hour of this, Frederick got up and went to talk to her. "Maybe he was just being polite" – Alex. "One is not polite to governesses" – Camille.

4.   She always looks up and smiles when he comes into the room. Always. Every time. She doesn't do it for anyone else. But she always does it for him.

5.   He sat for half an hour at breakfast just watching her. The Countess and Camille were arguing in French, Ruby and Alex were toasting bread on the fire, and he was just sitting there, drinking his chocolate. Not saying anything.

Just watching.

And then, on the third day...

Eleanor was sitting as usual in her seat in the corner of the drawing room. She was bent, as usual, over her sewing – not an elaborate dress for the Countess this time, but a darn in one of the stockings they had bought for Camille. Frederick had not protested at this – darning was apparently part of a governess's duties, and anyway, Eleanor liked to keep busy.

Isabella was talking loudly to the Countess about her trip to Bath last year. It sounded dreadfully boring to Alex – lots of balls, and walks, and being admired by young men. But if the Countess was bored, she was too polite to say anything. She sat as stiffly as a portrait, looking altogether too glamorous for Frederick's rough-and-ready English drawing room.

Frederick had been pretending to be interested in Isabella, but as she droned on, he looked more and more bored. Eleanor, as usual, was secretly watching him from under her eyelashes. She shifted position on the window seat, and her cotton reel slipped out of her lap and rolled on to the floor.

Frederick jumped up, picked it up, and took it across to her. "Your reel, my lady." She coloured slightly and took it. "I thank you."

On the other side of the room, Isabella was

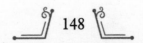

in full flood, telling a story about some awful-sounding ball.

"I often wonder what you're thinking, sitting so quietly here."

"I, think? Nay, governesses do not think, sir. We are not people. We are pieces of furniture, tables or chairs, hired for our usefulness, then discarded once we are no longer needed."

"You, not a person!" Frederick shook his head. "You are the most human creature I have ever had the good fortune to have met. Others are all artifice – but you! You are wholly yourself."

"No, not that!" Eleanor shook her head. "On the outside, I am all calm and reason, but inside! If you knew that girl, you would not admire her,

I think."

"I assure you, I would," said Frederick. "How could I not? You would think nothing cruel or wicked, I am sure of it."

On the table behind them was an arrangement of flowers. In amongst them were some little pink buds. One by one, slowly and silently, the buds were opening and the flowers uncurling. Alex watched in fascination. He wondered if anyone else had noticed.

"But there you are wrong. I feel such anger, sometimes. And I long for so many things."

"What do you long for?" said Frederick quietly. On the table, the flowers in the vase unclenched themselves, one by one by one.

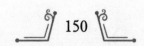

"Frederick! Frederick! What do you talk about so secretively in the corner?" It was Isabella. Both Frederick and Eleanor jumped. Isabella stood up very suddenly. She looked most put out. "I have a sudden fancy for a turn around the garden," she announced. "Frederick! Accompany me, if you will."

Frederick got to his feet at once, in a flurry of earnestness, and they left the room. Everyone looked at Eleanor.

"What was *that* about?" said Ruby.

There was a crash. The vase on the table had exploded, sending water and flowers spraying across the room.

"Oh!" said Camille.

"Was that *you*?" said Ruby. "Was that your magic?"

Eleanor bit her lip. Then she ran from the room

The children looked at each other.

"Come *on*," said Ruby, and she ran out of the door. Camille and Alex followed.

Isabella and Frederick were standing by the doorway, already mid-row.

"You must ask them to go!" Isabella was hissing. "They will never leave if you do not ask them! Are you to pay for her ladyship's wardrobe? Her maid? Her governess? Are you to buy her son's commission in the army?"

"I cannot simply throw her on to the parish!" said Frederick. He glanced up at the children as they passed, and looked quickly away. "We are

endeavouring to find her family…"

"You are? Or she is? And how is it you came to know her? Is she a dear companion of your early childhood? An old friend of your family? No! She is the merest acquaintance! You cannot say she knows *nobody* in England. Half the French aristocracy are here!"

"Indeed, and we are hopeful that we shall find –"

Eleanor was standing near the top of the staircase. She was staring down at the two figures in the hallway with an expression of fascinated horror.

"Are you OK?" said Ruby. "What happened down there? What were you and Frederick talking about?"

For a moment, Eleanor didn't seem to have heard. Then she came back to herself with an obvious effort.

"We should leave," she said. "It is not seemly to listen to others' private conversations."

"It's not seemly to have conversations at the top of your voice in the hallway," Ruby muttered. But she started to climb the stairs. The others followed.

Below them, Isabella was growing more hysterical. Had she forgotten that the Countess was in the drawing room? Or did she simply not care?

"I do not care where they go!" she shouted. "I

do not! I want them gone! All of them!"

"But, my dear—"

"What does it mean, this throwing on to the parish?" said Camille in a clear voice. Frederick glanced up the stairs. He seemed mortified by the whole situation.

"It means the workhouse," said Eleanor. She looked straight at Frederick as she said it, as though challenging him to deny it.

Frederick looked away, scratching the back of his head. He murmured, "Perhaps it might be better to continue this conversation outside, my dear…"

But Isabella would not be managed. She turned

on Eleanor, her face twisted in fury. "You!" she cried. "You ought to be ashamed of yourself. You think I don't see, but I see! Oh yes! I see everything!"

"Isabella! My dear!"

Eleanor held up her chin. Alex, watching, marvelled at the effort it was taking to control herself. She was trembling with barely contained emotion, but she did not speak or move.

Behind her, on the landing, a large ornamental vase began to tremble in time with Eleanor. Alex watched it in fascinated horror. Nobody but him seemed to have noticed.

Ruby, predictably, had no interest in holding her tongue. On the landing there were two sets of steps going upwards, one to the left, one to the right. Ruby was standing on the bottom of the right-hand steps, and she spun sideways in comic fury.

"You," she said, "are the rudest and most horrible person I have *ever* met. And I've met some horrible people!"

"Ruby!" said Eleanor, shocked.

Camille grinned. *"Mon Dieu!"* he said delightedly.

"It's not even your house!" said Ruby. "He isn't even your husband yet! And if we have anything to do with it, he won't be!"

"Frederick!" cried Isabella. "Are you going to stand there and allow me to be insulted like this?"

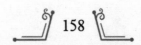

"Ah, well, naturally, I—"

"Tell her, Frederick! Tell them! Tell them they must leave! This instant! I insist!"

"Oh no, you don't!" shouted Ruby. She leaped down off the stairs on to the landing. The vase on the little table gave a wobble – from the jump or from some other power? – and smashed into a thousand pieces. Ruby landed awkwardly, stumbled, and – before any of them could catch hold of her, fell backwards, hitting her back with a sickening *crack* and bumped her way all the way down the staircase, landing in a crumpled heap at the bottom.

Where she lay still.

CHAPTER NINE
SELFISH
BONES

Alex stood at the top of the stairs. He felt frozen all over. He couldn't move. Neither, apparently, could any of the others. They stood like dolls in an old-fashioned puppet theatre, staring at her little huddled body. She couldn't… It couldn't…

Not Ruby... It wasn't...

"Good God!" said Frederick. He pushed past Isabella and ran towards Ruby. This seemed to release the others; Isabella, downstairs, began to have what sounded like hysterics.

"Oh! Oh! Oh! Poor creature! Poor child! She is dead, I am sure of it! Oh, lord! Oh, mercy! I feel faint! I cannot stomach it! Oh!"

The Countess appeared in the doorway to the drawing room. If she had heard the argument – and she could hardly have avoided it – she showed no sign of it. Her eyes went straight to Camille, at the top of the stairs. *Are you hurt?* He shook his head slightly.

"Enough!" It was Eleanor. She ran lightly down

the stairs and kneeled besides Frederick. "Can't you contain yourself, Isabella? There are children here!"

Alex still couldn't move. Ruby was lying very still, her body at an odd angle. She *wasn't* dead, was she? You couldn't die just from falling downstairs, could you?

Could you?

Frederick and Eleanor's heads were close together. They were talking in low voices.

"I do not think she is breathing."

"We must call for the apothecary at once," Frederick was saying. "But I fear..." He glanced up, saw Alex, and switched seamlessly into very accomplished-sounding French.

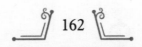

But Eleanor wasn't listening. She was looking at Alex and Alex was looking at her. There was a ringing in his ears. He gripped on to the bannister as hard as he could. He thought he was going to faint.

"Please wait," she said.

She stood up and walked up the stairs to Alex.

"Please," said Alex. His mouth was dry and it was hard to force the words out. "Please do something. Anything. Please help her."

"I will try," said Eleanor. "I do not know… I am not sure… But I will try. I promise."

Then she reached into her pocket and drew out the silver witch's bottle.

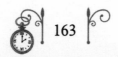

Some people live ordinary, happy lives doing more or less the same thing every day. Some people live lives full of marvels and adventures. Alex, you may already have guessed, was beginning to be one of the second sort of people. He lived a long and busy life, and in it, he went to many strange places, and saw many wonderful things.

But even when he was an old man, he never forgot that moment on the stairs of Applecott House. The Countess standing there in her long Versailles gown, her hair, still beautiful, tumbling down over her shoulders. Camille beside her in his silk stockings and little blue jacket. She looked like a queen, Alex thought. Outside the landing windows, the sun was beginning to set in glorious pinks and oranges, and it gave the pair an eerie, dangerous-looking backdrop, as though the whole world was burning.

And in France, of course, it was.

Perhaps Alex should have guessed what was going to happen next, but he hadn't. The sight of Ruby huddled at the bottom of the stairs seemed to have taken away his ability to think sensibly about anything. But perhaps some part of him already knew. In any case, he was not at all surprised when Eleanor lifted the bottle and held it to her mouth. Perhaps she said something; if so, Alex did not hear it. But he *felt* it, a shifting in the universe, exactly like, he realised suddenly, the feeling when you came through the mirror and landed in another place in history. At the bottom of the stairs Frederick lifted his head with a sudden jerk.

"Miss Crouchman!" he said. Then: "Eleanor! What do you there?"

Eleanor turned and smiled at him. There was a distant, almost blissful look in her eyes.

"Miss Crouchman!" cried Frederick. "I beg you – desist! Do not leave me! Eleanor!"

Eleanor's mouth opened. She tipped back her head, very slightly, and she almost – did she, or was Alex imagining it? – *did* she lift, very slightly, off the ground? Surely she didn't? And yet Alex was almost certain that he'd seen it, her neat grey slippers lifting off the stair.

And then – just as suddenly as it had begun – the magic was gone. Alex felt it like a jolt in his stomach – his hands instinctively gripped the bannister, to stop him from falling.

Above him, the Countess cried, "*Mon Dieu!*" and Camille said, "*Maman!*"

Below them, Isabella was still moaning.

"Oh! Oh, whatever is it? Is't witchcraft, I am sure of it!"

Eleanor was standing just as she had before, halfway up the stairs. Nothing about her had changed … but everything about her had changed. The faraway look in her eyes had gone. Whatever magic it was that had rushed through her – through them all – had gone. She still held the perfume bottle loosely in her hand.

"Gone," she said. Her voice was full of astonishment. "Gone! It's all gone! My magic – gone!"

"Miss Crouchman?" said Frederick tenderly. He took her hands. "Are you quite well?"

"Perfectly well," said Eleanor. Then she stumbled and seemed to slump against him in a faint. Frederick began to call out for wine. Isabella stopped her hysterics and glared at him.

But Alex didn't see what happened next. Because there was a movement at the bottom of the stairs. Incredibly, astonishingly, miraculously, Ruby was sitting up, saying, "Ow! What just *happened*?" And then, seeing all their astonished eyes upon her: "What did I miss?"

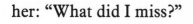

Everyone was talking. Isabella was shouting. The Countess was babbling away in French. Frederick was trying to get everyone to shut up, and nobody was listening.

Alex sat on the bottom step on the stairs and hugged Ruby so tightly he thought he would never let go.

"You were *dead*," he kept saying. "You *died*."

"I *know*," said Ruby. "You told me already. Keep your hair on. I'm alive now, aren't I?" But even she seemed shaken. Alex rested his head on her shoulder and the two of them sat there, listening to the commotion.

"T'was witchcraft!" Isabella was shrieking. "Devilry! That *woman* – she is not a woman! She is a demon in human form! Raising children from the dead! Seducing you away from me!"

The Countess gave a most unladylike bark of laughter.

"Eleanor, a seductress!" she said. "My! English womanhood is in a sad state indeed!"

Isabella glared at her. "That woman," she said. "She must go! Now! Tonight! Or I shall call for the constable! You are demons, all of you!"

"My dear," said Frederick, rather ineffectually. Like the Countess, Alex had a strong suspicion he was trying not to laugh.

"Demons!" she shrieked.

At this Frederick really did start laughing.

"Oh, I am sorry," he gasped. "I am sorry. But really! I! A demon! Oh!" And he doubled over again.

Isabella looked furious. "Oh!" she cried. "Oh! How could you? Abominable man! To think I ever fancied myself in love with you! You, sir, are a cad and a scrub and everything that is disagreeable! This engagement is over!"

She rose to her feet, shaking with fury.

"I hope you do not intend to remain in this parish, after this insult to my family!" she said. "I assure you, no one will wish to associate with you! You shall be quite alone!"

Frederick gave her a stiff little bow. She gave a rather formal bob in return, then swept out of the house. They heard the front door slam behind her. Then silence.

"Mr Pilgrim!" said the Countess.

Frederick looked a little abashed.

"That was exceedingly ungentlemanly," the Countess said.

"I am most sensible of it," Frederick agreed.

"And uncommonly rude," added Eleanor.

"Indeed it was." A small smile was twitching at

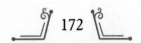

the corner of Frederick's mouth.

The Countess shot him a sharp look.

"Well!" she said. Then: "That notwithstanding, I cannot pretend to be sorry. I never met such a disagreeable girl in all my life."

Frederick looked up in surprise. Then, without warning, he began to giggle. Once he'd started, he didn't seem able to stop. He giggled and giggled and giggled, and the others, after a moment's surprise, joined in.

"But what of the living?" said Eleanor. It was later: tea and little cakes had been served, and they were all sitting in the drawing room together. "Miss Broderick is quite correct; without her good name, and the goodwill of her family, it will be difficult to make a life here. And it is very hard to live without friends. I should know."

Her voice was steady, but there was a stillness to her that made Alex wonder. What would it be like to be a governess in a great house like Versailles, to stay quietly in her rooms teaching Camille while all the grand ladies and gentlemen danced and feasted? Were there other women like her there? Were they allowed to talk to each other?

"Oh! As to that, I am glad of it," said Frederick. He rubbed his hands together in something that looked almost like glee. "For now I am free!"

"Free?" The Countess looked amused.

"Aye," said Frederick. "I was not made for a

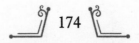

country parson. No, 'tis the high seas for me! Once our business here is all concluded, I'm for the royal navy, to make my way as chaplain. I wish I might go to New South Wales," he added dreamily. "And see kangaroos and wallabies and – oh! I long for it above all things!"

"New South Wales?" said Eleanor. "But is it not dangerous?"

"Excessively dangerous," said Frederick happily. His happiness was so contagious that Alex found himself grinning. New South Wales was Australia, wasn't it? He could just imagine Frederick on a ship somewhere, fighting pirates, singing sea shanties, landing on strange shores and eating kangaroo steaks and making friends with wallabies.

"It sounds brilliant," he said.

"Yeah," said Ruby. "But what about Camille and the Countess and Eleanor? What about them?"

"Do not be anxious on my behalf," said Eleanor. She looked at her hands. "I can provide for myself. It is Camille and the Countess you must concern yourself with."

Frederick stared at her. She lifted her head and looked back at him, her grey eyes steady.

"Well," said Frederick. He seemed suddenly flustered. "Well, I mean, yes, naturally you, evidently, you must—"

"Oh, for goodness' sake!" said Ruby. "Just ask her to marry you, can't you? You obviously want to."

Frederick went bright red.

"I – that is – Eleanor is – I'm sure she would not –"

"Of course she would," said Alex. "Are you completely mad? She thinks you're brilliant."

Frederick lifted his head. His eyes met Eleanor's in silent question, and now it was her turn to blush. The expression on Frederick's face was incredible – like a small child who thinks he's about to be told off, and is given a present instead. His chagrin turned to utter joy.

"Is't true?" he said. "You do not think me an utter jackanapes?"

Eleanor smiled. "Why, yes," she said. "Naturally, you are a jackanapes." Her expression softened.

"But it is true that I love you."

He came forward and took her hands. His voice was low and soft.

"And will you ... would you do me the very great honour of being my wife? I cannot promise you much. I am just a country parson, and one who is somewhat maligned at present. I do not know—"

"A country parson?" said Eleanor. "Do my ears deceive me? Are you not bound for a life of adventure on the seven seas?"

"Why, yes, but—" Frederick looked confused. "You would wish me to leave you?"

"Naturally not. But why should you leave me behind?"

"Mean you that – you would wish to come with me?"

"Beyond anything." Eleanor's eyes were shining. "Why! I went to Versailles to look for adventure. What is a little boating trip to the Antipodes compared to that?"

"My dear!" He took her hands. "It is somewhat more than a boat trip. There may be pirates, storms, kangaroos!"

"Why, yes! I long to see kangaroos above all things," said Eleanor. Her face was shining with happiness. She looked like quite a different person.

"Then I shall capture one and make it your especial pet," said Frederick. He took her hand.

"And you shall take it walking along the shore and feed it upon bananas and pineapples and all the fruits of the Antipodes."

"I don't think pineapples and bananas grow in Australia," said Ruby. But she was grinning too. "I knew you guys ought to be together! I told Alex – didn't I, Alex?"

"Yup," said Alex.

"I suppose congratulations are in order," said a voice behind them. It was the Countess. Alex felt a stab of guilt. Here they were talking about kangaroos, and they still hadn't found a home for Camille and the Countess. What was going to happen to them if Frederick ran off to Australia?

"Perhaps you two could go too..." he said

awkwardly. "Could Camille be a midshipman or something? They have kids on ships, don't they?"

"Indeed they do," said the Countess stiffly. "But midshipmen do not usually travel with their mothers. It is of no matter. We have troubled upon Mr Pilgrim's hospitality for too long. Perhaps one of Mr Pilgrim's charities will be able to find our relations. They cannot all have disappeared into the Bastille."

"Naturally, we will make every effort—" Frederick began, but there was a sudden shriek from behind Alex.

"*Maman!*"

It was Camille. His face had gone a greenish sort of white.

"*Regardez!*" he said. Then, as they stared at him, "Look! Look!"

He was pointing through the door into the hallway.

He was pointing at the mirror.

CHAPTER TEN
THE PILGRIMS
COME HOME

The reflection had changed. It now showed – Alex felt his heart jump – not the drawing room, but what looked like a warehouse. Various pieces of grand-looking furniture were lying higgledy-piggledy all over the floor, some in packing cases, some just sitting on top of each other.

"Why, that's Higson's in London!" said Frederick. "'Tis where I bought your looking glass—"

"*Mon Dieu!*" the Countess exclaimed. "*C'est Philippe!*"

A man had appeared in the frame. A grandly dressed gentleman, holding what looked like a jewellery case, and talking to another man who looked decidedly shabbier.

"Yes, look there, that's Higson – the auctioneer, you know. Capital fellow!"

But nobody was paying Frederick any attention.

"Oh!" the Countess moaned. "It is my brother, Philippe! He is in England! He escaped! But oh!

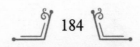

Mama's diamonds! He is selling them! I know he is! My dear Philippe!"

"But I do not understand," said Camille. "Why is the looking glass showing this to us now?"

"It's sending you home," said Ruby. "That's what happens to us when we've done whatever it is we're supposed to do. It just opens and sends us back where we're supposed to be. It's sending you back to when it was in the auctioneer's. It's found your brother for you. And his diamonds."

"But why did it not do so before?" said the Countess.

They all looked at Ruby and Alex. For a moment, neither of them knew what to say. Then Alex realised.

"Because we've done what we were brought here to do," he said. "We thought we were supposed to find a home for the Countess, but what if that wasn't it at all? What if we were supposed to get Frederick and Eleanor together – Mr Pilgrim and Miss Crouchman, I mean?"

"Oh!" said Ruby. "Oh, I bet it was! We did it, so now we can all go home!"

The Countess drew herself up in indignation. "Are you suggesting that I have been brought here as a–a prop in the idiotic romance of a governess and a parson?" she said.

"That governess saved your life!" said Ruby.

"Hush!" said Eleanor. "I do not mind her ladyship. She is right – it is excessively bewildering." She went over the Countess and gave a little curtsey. "My powers are outside all understanding," she said. "But it is *my* understanding that it always wished me good fortune – and good fortune to all my friends. I cannot countenance that it would ever believe your ladyship and his lordship to be props or..." She faltered.

The Countess's face cleared. "You are a dear, sweet child," she said. "Camille and I will be forever grateful to you. I wish you every happiness with your ridiculous suitor."

"Indeed, we will be the happiest souls alive," said Frederick. He grinned at them both. "I hope we may meet again sometime?"

"I think that exceedingly unlikely," said the Countess. She gave them a very formal bow. Camille did the same.

"Farewell, Mademoiselle Crouchman," he said. "I hope you will be very happy on your ship."

"*Au revoir*, Camille," said Eleanor.

The Countess took Camille's hand. She nodded to Alex and Ruby. And they stepped into the mirror, and were gone.

The Pilgrims – and the soon-to-be Pilgrim – were left alone in the hallway.

"Well!" said Frederick. He ran his hands through his hair, leaving it sticking up in impossible-looking tufts. "No one told me being a country parson would be so exciting!"

"Nor a governess," said Eleanor, smiling across at him.

"Thank you," Ruby said. "I never said it before but ... thank you. You saved my life. I'm sorry about your magic."

Eleanor shook her head. "I do not mind it," she said. "I am glad it is gone."

"How did you know what to do?" asked Alex curiously.

"I know not..." said Eleanor. "I simply saw your sister there, and as I grieved for her, I remembered your story of the witch in the bottle. And I wished with all my heart that I might put myself inside it, if it would save her, since it was I who brought her here, and so my fault that she was hurt. And then... Well, then you saw what happened then."

"Thank you," said Alex rather uselessly. *Thank you* didn't feel nearly big enough for all he felt.

"Pish!" Frederick was grinning. "It is us who must thank you. You have made us the happiest people alive."

"No worries." Ruby grinned back. "That's practically our job."

"What will you do with the bottle?" Alex asked curiously. Eleanor took it out of her pocket and looked at it.

"It stays in Applecott House, you say?"

"We will lock it up with our finest treasures!" said Frederick. "We will pass it on to our children's

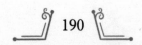

children and their children. Although … if we go adventuring, Applecott House will no longer be our home. It is a parsonage, you know, it shall go to the next parson."

"Maybe you come back here after your travels?" said Ruby. "Or maybe one of your great-grandchildren buys it or something. The Pilgrims honestly do end up living here, for years and years and years, I promise you."

"I am glad of it," said Eleanor. "'Tis a fine house, with a pleasant aspect. I should be sorry to think I should never see it again."

"And what will you do now?" said Frederick. "Will you be returning to the land of self-lighting candles?"

Ruby and Alex looked at each other.

"I dunno," said Ruby. "I hope so."

And they both looked at the mirror. And there, just as Alex had known it would be, was Aunt Joanna's familiar hallway.

"Upon my soul!" cried Frederick. "Is it not wonderful?"

"It is," said Ruby. "It's the most wonderful thing I've ever known."

"And you must let us thank you again!" Frederick said. "Our future happiness is all your doing! If we thanked you a thousand times, it would not be enough!"

"Seriously?" said Ruby. "Eleanor saved my *life*. If anyone has to thank anyone, it's us."

"It really is," said Alex. The memory of Ruby's body was still too close and too terrible to think about.

"My dear – just look!" Frederick peered into the mirror. "Two hundred years into the future! I wish you would take me through your looking glass, that I may see your future for myself. I wish you may – I would like it beyond anything!"

"Nay." Eleanor took his hand. "Not beyond *anything*. I am exceedingly fond of the future I have here."

They smiled at each other. Ruby made vomiting noises.

"Come on," said Alex. Then, to Frederick: "I suppose we ought to leave the clothes behind? If they were donated for poor people, I mean?"

"Alas, I think you must," said Frederick.

"We always do have to," said Ruby sadly. "And they'd be such good time-travel proof too. I feel like we ought to take a newspaper back or something, but they'd just think we bought it from the internet."

They took off their Georgian clothes, and redressed in their normal things. As always, their modern clothes felt strange and stiff, like a costume. Nothing was really warm enough, and they even smelled unfamiliar. Like home.

Downstairs, the mirror still showed Aunt Joanna's hallway. Eleanor curtsied to them, and Frederick bowed. Alex and Ruby did the same rather self-consciously.

Eleanor held up a hand as though to say goodbye. "Good luck."

"You too," said Alex. And they stepped through the glass.

The twenty-first century. Applecott House.

Home.

"Ow!" cried Ruby. Then: "Doesn't it feel weird to be back!"

It did. Applecott House looked simultaneously new – Aunt Joanna had had the whole hallway redecorated last month – and old. The bannisters looked dark and chipped, the window panes worn, the fireplace strangely grubby and cracked.

As ever, Alex found the too bright colours and too loud noises dizzying – the television in the bed and breakfast guests' sitting room, the lawnmower in the garden.

"Aunt Joanna!" Ruby shouted. She ran to the garden door and pulled it open. "Hey, Aunt Joanna! We did it again."

Aunt Joanna was halfway down the back lawn with the lawnmower. She looked up as the children came pelting towards her, and turned it off expectantly.

"1795!" Ruby shouted, running across the lawn towards her. "The French Revolution! Love amongst the hymn books! Life! Death! Stewed cucumbers!"

"Goodness me." Aunt Joanna brushed her hair out of her eyes. "Ruby Pilgrim, what *are* you talking about?"

"Time travel! Honestly, Aunt Joanna, weren't you listening? We went back in time, only this time it was all Georgian!"

"What? Oh, really, Ruby, not this again."

"Aunt Joanna, you are hopeless! What do we need to do? Next time I'm going to make sure I have my phone, and I'm going to take pictures of everything! I can't think why I didn't do it that first time."

"She'd just think we'd photoshopped them," said Alex gloomily.

Aunt Joanna laughed. "Dear, dear," she said.

"What sceptics you have for relations! Come on then, let's go back inside and you can tell me all about it."

The children turned to go, Ruby still arguing, her hands waving furiously in the air. Aunt Joanna watched her with affection. What a vivid child she was! Although ... she frowned. How in heaven's name had her neck got quite so dirty between now and this morning? Alex's was the same. What *had* they been playing at? Her frown deepened. That cut on her arm looked nasty. It had scabbed over already, but *surely* it hadn't been there at breakfast? Had it? Surely she would have noticed?

Wouldn't she?

They passed through the hallway and into the kitchen, where their mother was arguing with one of the roofers, and Aunt Joanna sat sipping her tea and listening as the children's story grew more and more convoluted. The hallway, for once, was empty and still. The bed and breakfast guests watched their television programme, a fly buzzed idly against the windowpane, but nothing else moved.

The mirror was silent, but the picture it showed was of another, older Applecott House.

This hallway was dim and tiled, in a rather sombre pattern of black-and-white tiles. There was a green umbrella with a duck's-head handle in the umbrella stand, a ration book on the table, and a Meccano model of a crane, half constructed and abandoned on the floor. The coats on the coat stand looked strangely old-fashioned, and so did the hats that hung on the hat-standy bit on top.

If anyone had been there to see and hear – but nobody was – they would have seen a little girl running past the mirror, in a brown coat, much darned, green gumboots, and pink knitted hat, gloves and scarf. There was snow on her boots and on her gloves, and she was crying.

She didn't look up as she passed the mirror. She ran, still sobbing, across the hallway, and away.

The picture rippled. The dim, old-fashioned hallway with the black-and-white-tiles was

gone. The mirror showed the plain old twenty-first century hallway, just as it always did. And Aunt Joanna, coming through a moment later to answer the telephone, noticed nothing out of the ordinary at all.